GREEN TEA, BLACK GUINNESS, RED WINE

CHAPTER ONE – FULLY FLEDGED CONSTABLE

'Delta 54, Delta 54, from Uniform over.'

'Uniform from Delta 54 send.'

'Delta 54 can you take details of a hospital message.'

'Uniform from Delta 54, roger, send.'

'Delta 54 can you inform Mrs Lilly Nixon, 18 Green Lodge, that her husband is ready for discharge from the Royal Victoria Hospital and will be available for collection from Ward 13, after fourteen hundred hours'

'Uniform from Delta 54, roger.'

Constable Des O'Dowd who was Delta 54 early shift, a walking beat in the County Antrim town of Carrickfergus, made a mental note of the message to be delivered. That Des felt he had the mental capacity to remember all of the vital elements contained within the message was testament to his denial of stupidity.

Des was a former Police Cadet with the Police Service of Northern Ireland, turning his back on life at the age of seventeen and a half years. He had graduated just over a year previously from the Police Training Centre at Garnerville, Belfast, a former Catering College that once attracted hordes of the great unskilled youth of Northern Ireland, and transformed them into dirty finger nailed, chain smoking, pastry chefs and fast order, microwave reheat food cooks. The Police Training Centre was not a building that lay testimony to the cherished memories of the many who had sacrificed their lives; it was less edifice and more educational eyesore. Many felt Des would have been more suited to attendance during its former existence.

He was now approaching twenty, and had recently completed a full probationary year of being mentored by senior Constables at Carrickfergus Police Station, none of whom recommended that he be allowed to continue further in a police career. Sickness levels among senior Constables at Carrickfergus Police Station reached its highest level during that year. Only police officers at the highest ranks in Carrickfergus Police Station failed to detect any correlation.

Des was formerly of the protestant religion, (because of his absent father who rapidly walked out on him and his mother shortly after Des started to walk rather less rapidly, and any mention of whom is forbidden), now a recently converted non-practicing Catholic, in a nascent Police Force that cast aside its seldom warranted reputation for religious intolerance for a veneer of religious acceptance and a 50/50 Catholic/Protestant recruitment policy. Des's mother, at heart an atheist, realised early on that Des would need some assistance in securing a long term, reasonably well paid job.

Many long serving Catholic police officers resented the political machinations that contrived to create the Police Service of Northern Ireland, and disliked the Northern Ireland version of McCarthyism that permeated every facet of day to day policing. Des, quite simply, didn't know any better.

Following the bewilderingly successful completion of Des's mentoring year, he was now unleashed, unaccompanied, on the unsuspecting public in the shape of call sign Delta 54, the walking beat that covered the Carrickfergus town centre area. It included the once picturesque Carrickfergus Castle and harbour, whose scenic backdrop was blighted some years earlier by the construction of a Cooperative Supermarket that attracted very few customers, (of whom there were even fewer car owning customers), with a vast car parking area as devoid of cars as it was trees, greenery, and any hint of environmental aesthetics. It was a great place for the local twelve to sixteen year old youths to gather, drink cheap Coop beer and vodka, attempt to procreate, fight, and vomit, although not necessarily in that particular order. William of Orange landed at Carrickfergus Castle and a plaque stands on site to commemorate that day. This irony was lost to Des, but served well the needs of a few fellow Catholic officers who used the insult as a reason for transfer to normalised areas, a long way from Carrickfergus, a town that did nothing to disguise its Loyalist bigotry.

To say that the Town Centre itself was unremarkable was an undeserved compliment. Everything Under a Pound shops competed with Discount Corner stores in a sea of graffiti coated stainless steel security shutters. The ubiquitous Wetherspoons public house on High Street was the busiest place in town. Churches of various denominations littered the town and provided a sporting spectacle on Sundays when church goers rushing for twelve thirty services competed on footpaths and roadways with hung over drinkers making for the opening of Wetherspoons welcoming front doors, and cheap but instant relief. It was an act of incredulity that the less than venerable town councillors had attempted to achieve 'city' status for Carrickfergus, a town lucky to hang on to its town status.

Des had paraded for duty at six forty five that Monday morning along with the other members of C Section. He had been with C Section for his entire mentoring year, apart from brief spells with Specialist Units as part of his learning experience. There were five other uniformed officers, four of whom manned the two mobile patrols that covered the outlying mix of middle class suburban sprawl and decrepit Loyalist housing estates, the other was a full time Reserve Constable who shared front gate security duties with a civilian security officer. One much older uniformed officer, Ronnie, manned the Station Enquiry Desk. They were led by Sergeant Alison Reid, a woman who did not like to do too much, as evidenced by her makeup and general appearance. Des got on reasonably well with everyone but was unaware that at times, lots of times, most of the time, his overzealous attempts to integrate and become accepted as a core member of C Section were interpreted by some, a lot, all but Des, as acts of stupidity.

Des got ready to leave Carrickfergus Police Station en route to 18 Green Lodge, part of the residential area between the Police Station and the town centre. He felt somewhat elated, confident that his contribution at breakfast in the canteen had served to cement his standing within C Section. It always amazed Des that on early shift, no matter what was happening; everyone had breakfast in the canteen after parading for duty. People simply queued in the Enquiry Office, calls were stacked up, and the fat boy breakfast took precedence.

May was the early morning cook. She disliked her job almost as much as she disliked her customers and saw no reason to disguise it. She looked around sixty five, sixty six, but was in fact only forty years of age. She had a square face, menacing forearms, and legs that would support any sumo wrestler. Her knuckles still bore the LOVE, HATE, lettering she had pin pricked into her hands by her first boyfriend. May was grumpy at most times of the day, but at this time of the morning in particular she was feared by most; except Ronnie, the Enquiry Desk officer, who had been first to order breakfast. When Des thought about it, Ronnie was always the first to get to the canteen on early shift.

Ronnie had served over twenty years in the Royal Ulster Constabulary before it became the Police Service of Northern Ireland so Des, as advised, tended to steer clear of one on one conversation with Ronnie. This was not something that was instructed explicitly during police training. Des of course was aware of the Royal Ulster Constabulary, and all the plaudits, condemnation and controversy that surrounded the forerunner of the Police Service of Northern Ireland. It was however tacitly imbued in Des and his fellow students during police training that the Royal Ulster Constabulary personnel still serving with the Police Service of Northern Ireland were representative of a distinctly different style of policing. Moreover, their experiences, and 'old school' methodologies and mind set could not fit in with the modern, transparent, divergent, style of policing adopted by the Police Service of Northern Ireland. 'Whistle blowing' was encouraged, but Des still had a deep seated respect and admiration for these people, without actually wanting to be seen as supportive in any way lest someone would blow the whistle on Des.

'Fondest salutations this fine morning May, it fills my heart with cheer to know that the sumptuous meal you are about to set before me will carry me through the days travails,' said Ronnie, without any suggestion of sarcasm.

'Fuck off Ronnie, and tell me what the fuck you want,' said May politely.

'Eggs Benedict with just the merest shaving of Italian truffle if it's in season please May.'

'Ronnie, you are doing my fucking head in already, and other fuckers are waiting.'

'Then just the fullest of fry ups please May while I wrestle with your intellect.'

'Wanker.'

Ronnie assembled the tables in the canteen so that the seven members of C Section sat together. Des loved this chance to let his colleagues get to know him better in the informal setting of the police canteen – but struggled hard to know the difference between interjection and seamless inclusive discussion.

Everyone had a plate of deep fried potato bread, deep fried soda bread, deep fried sausages, oven crisp bacon, deep fried mushrooms, pan fried eggs and three day old reheated beans. Ronnie and Sergeant Alison Reid were chatting as Des joined them; he was last at the table. The Sergeant was also long time Royal Ulster Constabulary, and she and Ronnie had a relationship that the others in C Section were not privy to. Ronnie called her Ali, never Sarge, Des simply could not understand it. Was it a lack of respect? No one ever pulled Ronnie to one side or admonished him. What exactly were the Royal Ulster Constabulary shared experiences that seemed to permit such audacious laxity. Des knew he had a lot more to learn.

Des, as he approached the communal tables, overheard Ronnie and the Sergeant talking about the recent Headquarters directive instructing removal of the memorial plaques commemorating the loss of three hundred and fifty lives of Royal Ulster Constabulary members during the 'troubles' from the police canteen wall. They ceased talking as soon as Des joined them. But Des thought he had sufficiently picked up the tone of the conversation, and this was his chance to prove himself worthy.

'In Chicago there is a policeman killed every forty two minutes, how crazy is that.'

At first there was only the stunned silence that normally greeted any of Des's pronouncements, which Des mistakenly interpreted as acceptance of what he had said. After the briefest of pauses came the unified response from most of the other uniformed officers.

'Fuck off Des.'

'Honestly, it's true, every forty two minutes. I am not saying it happens on the minute, but the amount of police killings over any given recent year indicate that a policeman is murdered every forty two minutes.'

'Des, that's like over thirty policemen a day killed on duty.'

'Well I'm not saying it's thirty every day, some may be well less, and others more, I would say the weekends would be higher.'

'Over two hundred police fatalities a week.'

'Well, yes, averaged out, and I suppose that includes off duty murders as well.'

'How do they find time for all the funerals, there can't be too many poor undertakers in Chicago?'

'At that rate very few must reach the age of retirement. You could call yourself a two month veteran.'

'Where on earth did you hear this crap Des?'

'My Uncle Ted was there a few weeks ago on business and got talking to a guy in the hotel bar,' and before he could add additional credence to support his statements there was a chorus of;

'Ah for fucks sake Des.'

Uncle Ted had been around for as long as Des could remember. He had been in the British Army in Northern Ireland in the late seventies. Des, probably because of his police training he thought, was able to gauge when Uncle Ted was about to visit. His mother's mood changed, she was uplifted, happier, and smelled all the time as if she had just had an aromatic bath. Des wasn't sure which side of the family Uncle Ted actually came from. Uncle Ted lived in England and travelled a lot. Des did not even know if he had any cousins. Any real discussion about Uncle Ted was forbidden. Ted did know an awful lot though and Des never doubted his word.

Des was aware that Ronnie and the Sarge had said nothing. Des knew that they thought he was right. That was what experience had taught them and in time would teach Des. He was undeterred by the comments of the other members of C Section as he got up to prepare to leave and deliver the hospital message.

'Nice one Oedipus' Ronnie whispered, not for the first time.

Des kept on forgetting to do a google search on Eedipiss, he made another mental note.

Des checked himself out in the full length mirror in the locker room. He was five feet eleven inches but with his heeled boots and uniform hat looked way more than the six feet plus that he craved to be. He was fourteen stone and struggling to keep his weight down. He looked closely at his face, now approaching twenty one years of age, and detested the join the dot freckles that became highlighted when he blushed or his face reddened when engaged in physical exertion. Des was always more likely to suffer from the former. Des picked his nose a lot. He had given up the habit as a child when told by his mother that his head would cave in. He had resumed the habit with gusto in his early teenage years. Des would almost always closely examine and then eat what he managed to excavate from his freckled nose. If his nose had been bleeding Des didn't eat what he had picked, that would have been disgusting. If he was in the midst of a bad cold, and coughing up the most disgusting mucus and phlegm, he would of course have a cursory look, maybe a bit of a check on the texture by rolling same between his fingers, but digesting, mostly, absolutely not.

Des had rules and he proudly stuck by them, except occasionally, well frequently in respect of one particular sinful act. He had tried to stop masturbating for some years now. He dispelled the myth that it might make him blind some years ago; he was nonetheless worried that it may in some way affect his health. He was an avid practitioner of the 'anywhere and at any time' method. This particular method carried with it certain obvious dangers. He was naturally terrified of being caught, but when the impure thoughts took hold, common sense took second place to desire.

He loosened his leather holster belt by one hole, the fifth such extension in a year, and practiced a quick draw in the mirror. His issue firearm was a Glock nine millimetre pistol. He longed for the Ruger 357 Magnum revolver that many of his colleagues carried, but during firearms training the use of that particular weapon scared him. Each time he fired the weapon the recoil bruised the fleshy area between thumb and trigger finger. The noise deafened him, even when he wore two sets of protective ear defenders. Such was his fear and anticipation of both these events that instead of employing a smooth, controlled trigger action he rushed at it clumsily while simultaneously closing his eyes. Even the most fervent anti gun lobbyist would know that to close your eyes when firing a lethal barrelled weapon can have potentially lethal consequences for anyone within the range of that firearm – in any direction. The safest place to be when Des was on the firing range trying to tame the Ruger Revolver was probably in front of the target. Des had to settle for the more sedate Glock, not the Dirty Harry weapon of choice, but lethal nonetheless. He would keep his right arm over the holster as he walked so no one could see that he only carried a Glock.

His trousers wore knife edge creases, as did his green uniform shirt. His mother did the ironing and would not have it any other way. He decided not to wear the black kevlar body armour over his shirt, the choice was his, and Carrickfergus senior police officers liked to convey an aura of normality policing in the town. In truth the weight of the body armour tired Des, and the aroma of the thousands who had used it before him was so ingrained into the fabric that it made him wretch, as it would any but the totally insensitive or smell sense deprived . When Des's mother insisted that Des wear body armour at all times, Des would remove the kevlar plates from the velcro fastened compartments in the vest. Des then in effect patrolled in a smelly, black waistcoat, incapable of preventing the penetration of a rolled up newspaper. Ronnie, whose job it was to sign out the body armour quickly stopped issuing body armour to Des, and Des understood why.

Des knew his route lay along the sea front from the Police Station. It was a nice but windy day and Des did not want a repeat of the fiasco some weeks earlier when he approached a number of youths drinking cider on a promenade bench in contravention of local bye-laws. As Des approached, drawing himself up to his full height, having rehearsed what he was going to say, the wind blew his hat off, sending it nearly one hundred yards up the promenade. The cider drinking crowd laughed hysterically. Des now lacked inches in height as well as command of the situation, and knew he had to recover his hat in order to enforce his authority. He walked towards the hat as it moved nervously in the wind. As he bent down to pick it up a gust of wind blew the hat into the choppy waters of Belfast Lough. The hysterical laughter some seconds earlier would amount to nothing more than a smirk when compared against the convulsive seizure that now gripped the youths. Des had walked back without hat, but purposefully, to the police station. At the same time he played over a different scenario in his mind;

'Okay you scumbag, fuck pigs, let's see a star position by the railings, arms and legs outstretched,' Des would have said, the .357 magnum 'widow maker' drawn, and pointing at the seven youths that were just about to make his day.

'Fuck sake, we are only having a wee cider.'

'I know what you fuck pigs are thinking; there are seven of you and only six rounds in my chamber.'

'Just let us go man; we can all be cool and never come back here.'

Des did wonder why so many Americanisms had entered the local language, never mind the jeans hanging off the arse, and bloody skate boarding. He would remain true to his roots.

'The truth is, I can plug two of you mo fo's with one round, job done dog breaths.'

Before Des knew it he had walked past the police station, heading in the direction of Eden village, a place that could not be more undeserving of that particular name. Hades would be more suitable. He looked around him and with no one in sight he picked his nose, liked what he saw and ate it, and headed back towards the police station.

Des this time avoided the exposed promenade, and walked instead past the rows of terraced houses, and shops leading towards Green Lodge and the town centre. The aroma from Bewleys coffee shop drifted towards him, a blend of coffee beans and chocolate that Des was powerless to resist. Des popped his head through the open door; this was normally Des's first stop off point, barely three hundred yards from the police station.

'Morning Betty, caffeine fix in about fifteen minutes, got a quick call to make.'

'Okay son, double chocolate brownies are to die for today.'

Des's stomach was still struggling to cope with the two pieces of soda bread, two pieces of potato bread, three sausages, four rashers of bacon, eggs, beans, past expiry date mushrooms, glutens and saturated fat. Betty's words may have unwittingly conveyed more than just a literal translation. He did need his coffee though. The coffee in the police canteen was weak and insipid, unlike May who prepared it, and who was rumoured to add bodily fluids of the most disgusting variety. Des was aware he had piled on weight since joining the police force, and told himself he needed nothing further to eat that day. He would wait until his mother made dinner. It was Monday, and Monday meant chilli con carne.

As Des walked towards the town centre his ear piece crackled into life;

'Delta 54, Delta 54 from uniform.'

'Uniform from Delta 54, send over.'

'Delta 54 can you take details of a death message.'

'Uniform from Delta 54 roger, send over.'

'Delta 54 can you inform Mrs Ina Robinson, 22 Lawyers Lane, that her husband died at 0730hr this morning, Ward 6, Royal Victoria Hospital. He had been ill for some time and a death certificate has been granted, she needs to contact the ward sister.'

'Uniform from C54 roger that.'

Des made another mental note while he thought about the route to take. He would go to Lawyers Lane first and get the bad news dealt with before going to Green Lodge and then a well deserved coffee.

As he walked towards town Des could just see the Ulster Bank sign at the start of High Street. There was a small lane that ran between the shore car park and the start of High Street, and Des used to conceal himself there, as best as any green uniformed policeman could, hoping that an armed robber would emerge, bags of swag in hand, ensuing exchange of gunfire, Des the hero. That would be to fast forward somewhat in Des's mind. For sure he wanted the accolades and awards that go with such an act of heroism, but he could not quite resign himself to dealing with any possible physical injury to self. Even the most fleshy of flesh wounds bleed, and he was not quite sure, well absolutely sure actually, that he would not cope well with the sight of his own blood. He was not even sure how he would cope with the sight of any blood. At the Police Training College class visit to Foster Green

Mortuary during his training he fainted from the aroma when he entered the administration office. He remained comatose for so long that fellow students thought he may appear as the next cadaver. But still Des allowed his mind to think about bank robbery and heroism. His mind drifted. He did not recall his route, he ran through the many different scenarios leading to his greatness and total acceptance, almost legendary status. He was in Des world.

Suddenly, and with no recall of how, Des arrived at Green Lodge. He shook his head violently in a 'for fuck sake wake yourself up' sort of way, almost like pressing the refresh button, and made towards number 18. Green Lodge was a mix of maisonette type dwellings and flats for retirees. This was a last stop prior to residential care for many of the residents, the children of whom had wisely decided to manage any inheritance money lest the government should steal it. Des found the ground floor flat at number 18 without any difficulty. Pot plants stood proudly outside, and the wooden front door exuded years of unnecessary care and attention. A bird feed sleeve was hung next to a faux swiss cuckoo clock with wind chimes. Des wondered about the bird interaction here at certain times of the day, but the inability of his mind to progress beyond the merest detail hindered him in taking the thought process any further. It was what it was, and maybe as Des became more experienced he would understand why.

Des pressed the door bell, and heard the unmistakable muted tune of 'The Sash' from behind the door. A song that was originally intended and received as a tribute to Ulstermen who had fought in both wars, and now regarded as nothing more than a sectarian Loyalist diatribe, only the chorus of which is now regurgitated, 'ad nauseam' by drunken loyalist youths following once proud Orange Bands on parade.

'Hello son, come on in, sorry about the bloody bell, Jim's choice, he's a True Blue so we have to put up with it.'

Mrs Nixon was in her late sixties, with a wrinkled face that only a lifetime of smoking could provide, and the severest plastic surgery eradicate. She pointed Des towards the living room, and as he entered he was enveloped by the cigarette smoke that was visible in the room almost like a fog.

'Mrs Nixon, I think we need to get the kettle on, so let's get into the kitchen shall we.'

Des had been with one of his mentoring officers in delivering a death message, and the cuppa tea in the kitchen was the softened and successful strategy that he had applied.

'Of course son, are you here about Jim.'

'I'll just fill the kettle; you get the cups and tea bags Mrs Nixon.'

'He's a silly old bollocks, trying that ten pin bowling lark and getting himself a bloody hernia.'

The tea brewed, Mrs Nixon insisted on cup and saucer, as if this was how tea was normally drunk at number 18.

'Mrs Nixon, I am afraid that I have the job of delivering some very bad news to you. Unfortunately your husband died this morning at the Royal Victoria Hospital and you have to contact the ward to arrange to collect the death certificate and let them know about funeral arrangements. I am so sorry for your loss.'

Mrs Nixon met the floor before the contents of the upturned cup of tea. Des shot to the floor, well more that he allowed his weight to propel him there when he leant forward, and ushered Mrs Nixon back to a semi seated position. Her face was drained, her eyes glazed as she muttered;

'How can that be, how can that be, it was only a simple operation.'

'Mrs Nixon, the trouble with improvements in medicine now if you ask me is that so much can go wrong with the basics while the focus is on the highbrow stuff.' This was another line that Des had remembered from his mentoring officer.

'Oh god, how am I going to tell the family, they are going to be so shocked?'

'Just one step at a time Mrs Nixon, allow yourself time to come to terms with this, and then move onto the next step. Here are the contact details, and please dear, don't hesitate to contact me at any time if you need some assistance. Is there anyone close by can come and sit with you while I leave.'

'I think I'd rather be on my own for a while.'

You've got the rest of your life for that, thought Des.

'Okay Mrs Nixon, now let's finish our tea, you don't have any biscuits do you?'

Des had stayed on at Mrs Nixon's longer than he had expected, but in his undeniably limited experience in times of grief such as this, time should not be measured. A job well done, he moved onto Lawyers Lane.

Lawyers Lane was a small development of four storey apartments for housing the elderly, and only a short walk from Green Lodge. This was certainly the area of town where retirees came to retire and then die.

Number twenty two was on the ground floor, and the communal entrance front door was propped open with a fire extinguisher. Des nonetheless pressed the intercom button for the Robinson apartment to announce himself.

'Come on in Constable, I have been expecting this all day.'

Mrs Robinson was easily in her eighties; with a face that appeared as if it had bore witness to so much that nothing in the future could possibly present a challenge. She motioned Des through to the small square living room that was furnished in exactly the same manner as everyone over seventy years of age seemed to opt for. There must be an Ikea for the Aged store somewhere that Des was unaware of. The living room smelt of old people. Des had nothing whatsoever against old people, but the aroma was unmistakable. It wasn't offensive, or an indication of poor personal hygiene, it was just there. It certainly wasn't a fragrance that would make the top ten of Debenhams perfume department.

'Constable I'm telling you son, it's been a long hard road for all of us, especially my Peter. They'd have put a fucking dog down rather than let the animal endure that agony.'

Des was still slightly taken aback when someone so old and demure could resort readily to swear words.

'Well Mrs Robinson, the good news is that the wait is now over.'

'Yes, and praise the Lord, for all the fucking good he did.'

'Your husband is ready for collection at Ward 13, just let the ward know when someone will be there for him, I have written the number down here for you.'

For only his second occasion, but in a very short time from the first, Des knelt to assist in bringing the prostrate Mrs Robinson to a seating position.

'Constable are you sure, my Peter has been on deaths door for the last six months, and he looked like a fuck all squared corpse when I saw him two days ago.'

'Mrs Robinson let me tell you, the improvements in the science of medicine over the last few years has been nothing short of miraculous in terms of the amount of lives now saved by new techniques. It's amazing; we are all going to live into our hundreds the way things are going.'

'Dear God I take back all the nasty things I may have said through anger, the truth is you fucking did it. Constable, this is going to make a lot of people so, so, happy, and fucking amazed quite honestly. Thank you so much son.'

Des was almost tearful as he left Mrs Robinson's apartment. As he walked towards his well-deserved coffee at Bewleys he imagined himself as the much sought after Consultant

Surgeon that saved Peter Robinson's life. The sweat forming on his forehead being wiped away by a not unattractive Philippines theatre nurse;

'Scalpel please Sister.'

'Mr O'Dowd, no one has ever successfully completed this incision, are you sure?'

'A man's life is at stake Sister, and that means more than my reputation.'

Junior Doctors and experienced theatre staff alike swooned. The silent clock on the operating theatre wall could be heard ticking away the seconds.

The surgeon's hands moved majestically in manoeuvres that all those present would remember as the nadir in their surgical careers. They would feast in great glory at dinner parties as they endlessly recounted the feats witnessed at the hands of the great Mr O'Dowd.

'Stitch him up Sister, we are done for today, and this man can look forward to a healthy and lengthy retirement.'

Everyone present applauded, some would later recount that this included the heavily sedated patient. Des had allowed himself to forget that the origins lay in a simple hernia procedure, in a roundabout sort of way.

Des entered the coffee shop, once part of an ice cream parlour chain, that recruited a company of management consultants and researchers to establish why their expanding chain of ice cream parlours in Northern Ireland were failing to make any profits. To summarise the management company's final report after months of arduous research; ice cream only really sells for three months of the year, so diversify into beverages, chocolates, cakes and other random items of produce that are cheap to produce and easy to sell at a profit. Three years on and the resulting increase in profits came tantalising close to covering the management company's fees.

'Hi Betty, a double cream special please, four brown sugars.'

'Where have you been Serpico, another murder solved.'

'Can't really tell you, busy though, Christ the night it's nearly lunchtime already,' said Des looking at the clock above the shop till.

'And I thought you were a good catholic boy Des.'

Betty was about the same age as Des's mum, but with a truly fantastic figure. Well in reality it was a figure that was manipulated by being stuffed into the tightest possible clothing. For Des it was simply magnificent, a joy to behold forever. Today Betty wore the tightest white trousers that bulged without embarrassment in certain areas, and a low cut sheer pink top. As she walked away to get the coffee Des could see the black g string knickers, stretched to breaking strain, under the white trousers. It resembled a piece of black dental floss being drawn through a mouth of the whitest teeth. As she walked towards Des he could hardly take his eyes of her slightly wrinkled but magnificent cleavage pouring out of the undersized, ill fitting, black lace bra.

'What about a couple of the double chocolate brownies with whipped cream Des, you're a growing boy you know.'

'Betty I really shouldn't, I just finished some chocolate biscuits before I came here.'

Betty was sitting in front of Des now, her hand on his knee, pencil in hand, ready to take his order, her cleavage his sole focus of attention. If Betty went to fetch the brownies Des would get a repeat performance.

'Betty you are an awful woman, you have talked me into it, go on then.'

As Betty walked towards the kitchen area Des rubbed his hand over his trousers feeling his penis getting erect. He looked around the inside of the coffee shop urgently to make sure there was no close circuit television cameras fitted. The urge was taking over like an uncontrollable force within him. Did he have a Jekyll and Hyde personality disorder that framed his sexual appetite from now on until sated? He had just got himself so fucking horny. He could feel his face turning purple with embarrassment, something he simply could not prevent, and that Betty could not fail to see when she returned from the kitchen.

'Betty, Betty, have to come, I mean go, urgent radio message just come in.'

'At least finish your coffee Des,' she shouted from the kitchen.

Des was on his way out of Bewleys, his hands in his trouser pockets working furiously to disguise his erection. Des told himself he needed help, but first he would recount Betty's movements in his mind in the toilets at the police station before heading to the canteen for a late lunch. He was really annoyed he had missed the double chocolate brownies with whipped cream, but mistakenly convinced himself he had shown extreme discipline in doing so.

He checked his 'admin' tray after lunch, and to his delight he found an internal memorandum from the Sub Divisional Commanders office in Newtownabbey, approving his secondment to C.I.D. for three months beginning the 1st of June. It even bore the signature of Superintendent Brett Mayne. Des felt that his day could not possibly get any better. Here was a chance for Des, starting in just over three weeks' time, to prove himself worthy of consideration of appointment to C.I.D. as a probationary Detective. This was where Des saw himself; he had three months in which to showcase his analytical, investigative, and reasoning skills, his adeptness in persuasive and penetrating interviews of suspects, and caring yet productive interview techniques for victims. Des knew his mother would be proud of him, and probably want to buy him a few more suits to go with his Sunday best.

CHAPTER TWO – DETECTIVE CONSTABLE PETER SMYTH

Peter woke up without opening his eyes. There was no need for him to glance at the bedside alarm clock, as he woke every morning between five thirty and six o-clock, drunk or sober No matter how hard he tried to get back to sleep, it simply did not work. When awake, he was wide awake. In fairness Peter was very rarely either completely drunk or sober, he always found that middle ground, but occasionally edging more towards drunk than sober. He remembered brushing his teeth and sloshing the Listerine mouthwash before going to bed, but still the inside of his mouth resisted opening. It took no small amount of determined pressure before he was able to prise open his lips and inhale.

Eyes still closed he tried to recount the events of the late evening before. He had decided to stop off at Whitehead Golf Club which lay on his way home to Islandmagee, nothing more than a village of around five hundred people, with two general stores and a post office. Whitehead itself was a former small retiral village that had grown slowly into a small town. He had only popped in, ostensibly, to check his starting time for the next day's Saturday Social Four Ball. It was nearly ten o-clock, and a night cap on the way home seemed good sense. He had made an excuse to his long suffering girlfriend that he could not spend the night with her in Belfast; he just wanted a night on his own, again. For a man who exhibited signs of exclusion and awkwardness in social surrounds, he secretly desired company, even of the most banal nature. He preferred not to be in the social company of police officers, so the golf club met most of his social interaction criteria. The usual mix of suspects was in the members bar;

'Columbo what the fuck time is this, get the boys a drink, you were supposed to be here at fuckin six,' Facey shouted out above the din.

The 'boys' still did not appreciate that Peter did not work a normal eight to four routine, but tried to as best as he could. He looked around the bar, a mix ranging from unemployed, to builders labourer (but still claiming unemployment benefit), to teacher and architect. The common bond for Peter was the bonhomie and unified joy in the consumption of alcohol without resort to conversation about police activities. Peter found most police officers acutely boring outside of the work environment, and some boring enough in the workplace.

All of the guys had nicknames, known by everyone in Whitehead and Islandmagee, but requiring of explanation and translation anywhere beyond. Peter's nickname however did not require too much by way of explanation and he often wished to be re-nicknamed with a more obscure and thought provoking nickname.

'Some of us have to work 24/7 Facey you lazy fuck, I'll have a gin and tonic thanks.'

'Ah fuck, we will all sleep safer in our beds tonight knowing that Columbo has put in the extra hours,' chirped Spit in the Chips.

Peter always thought that by way of obviousness Spit in the Chips easily outshone Columbo.

Lenny owned the Whitehead Bakery. A former chef, he had set up the very popular bakery some three years previously, and put in very long, early morning starts, to ensure its continued local success. When pissed on a night out with the 'boys' in Whitehead the last port of call was normally the Chinese or Fish and Chip shop for a carry out. Lenny would always demonstrably spit into his carry out to deter the unwelcome hands of those too lazy, or too broke to buy their own. For Peter this was a no brainer. How could anyone hearing this nickname not know that this was why Lenny attracted that particular sobriquet?

'You should be in your fucking bed Spit in the Chips. Don't want any drunk hands doing the rolling of the fine pastry early in the morning now, do we,' retorted Peter.

'I have the morning off, bringing in Mary for the early shift, halle fucking lujah.'

'Spit in the Chips' possessed the undesirable skill of being able to punctuate standard, every day words, with swear words for added effect. Peter fluctuated between admiring this as a skill and simply ignoring it as crass use of the English language.

'I suppose that fucking early shift starts in your bedroom while she hand massages a template for the hot dog sausages,' shouted 'Arnie the Architect.'

This was followed by jeering and jibes from nearly everyone present except Mary's husband. He was the only person in the bar who did not know, or would not admit to, that Spit in the Chips was fucking his wife. He was not part of the core 'nickname' team, despite numerous failed sycophantic attempts to reach out to all concerned. He remained on the periphery, hoping that one day he too would be labelled and become part of the team. The consensus however was that anyone so thick as to not realise Spit in the Chips was fucking his wife was not worthy of consideration, merely condemnation and silent ridicule.

A very large gin and tonic appeared on the bar for Peter; he assumed had been bought by Facey. Some present were obviously more inebriated than others, and Peter drifted through the crowd towards a table where he could see 'Wardrobe,' and 'Necro' sitting. They appeared unusually sober and sensible, and exactly the type of company Peter needed as he embarked on only his first drink of the day. He didn't count the two double gins he had drunk from the stress relief cupboard in the North Queen Street CID office as he finished up his handover debrief, and incident report writing before leaving for Whitehead. The stress cupboard was in fact a secure documents cupboard, the innards of which had been removed and replaced with a gantry containing optics for gin, vodka and whisky, and a small fridge that contained beer and mixers. Everyone knew of its existence, but as the consumption of alcohol was forbidden inside police station buildings it was understandably kept under lock and key.

Only detectives serving in the office had keys, and an honestly policy was adopted whereby drinks consumed were entered onto a bar chit, signed by the recipient, and totalled at the end of each month when each would receive a bar bill. More forged signatures were applied than a handwriting expert in the Fraud Squad would be likely to encounter in his thirty year career. In some inexplicable way it more or less balanced out over the course of a year, as each detective who discovered a chit in his name, but clearly not his signature, would apply the signature of another detective to his own chit by way of recompense.

The gins consumed at work didn't seem part of the equation in his mind. It was merely a light remedy accompaniment following another arduous day.

'You two look remarkably sober and serious for a Friday night,' said Peter as he drew up a chair and joined them at the formica table.

'Wardrobes fucking wife is leaving him, again,' said Necro derisorily.

'His wife's always bloody leaving him but never does Necro.'

'It's different this time Columbo, I really have kicked the fucking arse out of it this time.'

'So she caught you pissing in the wardrobe again.'

Wardrobe was an electrician who had maintenance contracts with the only two pubs in Whitehead as well as the Yacht Club. In essence this provided only four to five hours of paid work each week, but Wardrobe liked to spend four to five hours of each working day between the three client establishments, thus ensuring them a first class service, and him a steady supply of Guinness that his wife was unaware of.

Wardrobe was in his early thirties and married to Jane, some fifteen years his senior. They had two daughters, Chloe aged nine, and Berry a recent unplanned, but welcome arrival of three months.

Wardrobe made a habit out of a terribly unsocial act that only a very small fraction of adult males seldom commit, and of those guilty, most would never admit to. When waking in the night from a drink fuelled stupor he would be unable to navigate his way around the bedroom in the dark to find either the door to the en suite bathroom, or a light switch to assist in his search. He would be overtaken by a primal fear, and a bladder full to overflowing thanks to the accumulation of ten to twelve pints of Guinness. His palms would feel out the bedroom walls in a frantic manner in search of the holy grails; toilet door or light switch. When unsuccessful he would happen upon the wardrobe, his oasis in the desert, hardly analogical given the circumstances. The wardrobe door was his toilet door, and the unsurpassed relief he felt when pissing into the wardrobe matched a sexual climax that only men who exhibited similar behavioural patterns can appreciate. Most of the time his wife Jane remained in the arms of Morpheus, and would only detect signs of his behaviour the next morning when finding the unmistakeable aroma and pool of urine on the wardrobe base, or urine staining across her hung clothes if Wardrobe had gone for the zig zag piss instead of the straight down method.

'Oh fuck I have done it this time mate, about twelve pints of guiness last night, and then that fucking poteen, that just done my brain in,' said Wardrobe as if presenting a defence for his actions.

Poteen is an illicitly brewed Irish spirit consisting mainly of potato skins and raw distilled alcohol. Occasionally fruit is added during fermentation to disguise its disgusting medicinal alcohol taste. It was the drink of choice for poor alcoholics, and factual reports exist of its power to render imbibers blind, strip stubborn paint from wood surfaces, and rid infertile fields of all manner of weeds and pestilence. Who on earth would want to consume such a lethal cocktail – certainly a few from the Darwin's waiting room that was Whitehead.

'I got home around midnight, Jane and the kids asleep, and had to have that bloody poteen nightcap. Next thing I remember is Jane screaming at me, and the bedroom lights going on. I was bloody pissing over Berry in her cot at the end of our bed. It was fucking flowing out, even with Jane fucking screaming and slapping me it took a while to stop.'

'Bloody hell Wardrobe, the child could have drowned, that's a new form of water boarding,' said Peter, incredulously, reminding himself that although he thought he had witnessed all of life's strangest behaviour, he could still be amazed by some of the Whitehead residents.

'That's worse than the time Jane and Chloe came home and found you wanking to Dancing on Ice in front of the television.'

'Don't need you to tell me that Columbo, killing my own bloody daughter by pissing on her would not have been well received by the extended family circle, there was never any need to tell the whole family about the accidental wanking, so they never found out about that.'

'Why the fuck was it accidental,' asked Necro.

'I was watching the wrong fucking channel you bloody nut.'

'So what's the latest,' asked Peter, trying to steer the conversation back to relative normality.

'Jane's taken the kids to her sisters in Belfast for the weekend and I need to have a working plan for self-improvement by Sunday or she is off to London with the kids, and she fucking means it this time.'

An air of silent contemplation fell over the table. Together a solution would need to be found for Wardrobe who appeared to spend half his life wishing Jane would leave with the kids, and the other half in begging her to stay. It was going to be no easy problem to solve. The Guinness overfilled Wardrobe's bladder, and poteen turned him into an uncontrollable monster. Without the poteen Wardrobe still had episodes of toilet and light panic, and pissed anywhere in the bedroom. Could the answer be to cut out the high volume beer and stick to spirits? Poteen may turn him into an uncontrollable monster, but a monster nevertheless without a bladder that required immediate emptying. There was a lot to ponder over the next day's golf, and as the three sat studiously at the formica table a call broke the silence.

'Just received word of a worldwide juniper berry crop failure,' yelled Arnie the Architect, standing unsteadily atop a table in front of the bar. 'Surplus stores have all been used up; they reckon that there will be no gin production for at least two years.'

Nervous husbands could be seen looking at their watches and routes towards the exit doors. Could they manage a covert exit? Their wives wrath at arriving home late, and inebriated, was nothing compared to the embarrassment, and ridicule, of being caught trying to sneak out of the club. Almost in unison that any Welsh male choir would have been proud of came the guttural cry;

'Gin, gin, gin, gin, gin.'

If a sound recordist were later to eradicate the shouts of gin, a few muffled appeals of 'oh fuck no,' and 'that's me fucked,' would have been detected. Juniper berry crop failure calls were made at least twice a month, with disastrous effects not for the juniper berry crop, but the assembled gin drinkers in Whitehead.

Peter lay in bed and estimated he had drunk a further six or seven double gins before getting into his car for the short drive to Islandmagee. No problems were encountered; he felt he drove exceedingly better after a couple of drinks, believing that the alcohol sharpened his senses and awareness. He resisted his normal habit of having a nightcap. He knew this inevitably led to a three a.m. wake up on the living room settee with a stiff neck, and he wanted to feel as fresh as he could for golf on Saturday.

He had walked from the living room down the hallway leading to his bedroom, and passed the studio photograph of his wife and daughter, aged thirty nine and twelve at the time, murdered by an under car booby trap bomb, planted by the IRA and intended for Peter, less than a year after sitting for the photograph. He brushed the surface of the photograph with the fingers of his right hand as he passed, and cried himself to sleep in bed. His nine year old daughter was identified from dental records, and his wife from jewellery found at the scene. He blamed himself for allowing his wife to swap cars with him. She had no water in her windscreen washers and so took his car that fateful day. He should have filled that washer bottle each day she moaned at him to do so. She would have laughed at him if he had told her to check underneath the car for devices each time she used it.

It was nearly ten years since he lost his wife and daughter but the pain never subsided. It gripped him, and made him physically sick when he dwelled too long on the minute detail. He imagined the noise from the detonator cap that they would probably not have heard, followed instantly by the impact of the high explosives contained within the large Tupperware container attached inside the front passenger wheel well, filled with ball bearings, screws, and pieces of barbed wire. Individually each of these metal objects became lethal as they ripped through the flesh and bones of his wife and daughter. He hoped that the blast lung damage brought an early fatal relief before the impact of the flying metal debris. The subsequent inferno removed all traces of humanity. He never got to see his wife and daughter for one last time in peaceful, serene, repose, their bodies discreetly covered by crisp white sheets on a mortuary table; their eyes and mouths gracefully angelic thanks to the work of the mortuary attendant. Even that had been denied him, and he fought hard to contain his anger.

Peter had joined the Royal Ulster Constabulary in 1982, following in his father's footsteps, as was fairly common in those days. In 1986, in what some considered a very short time, he achieved his goal of becoming a C.I.D. Detective, based at North Queen Street Station in the Irish Republican New Lodge area. Peter was indifferent as far as religion was concerned. To him a terrorist was a terrorist, regardless of background, religion or creed. He did however agree with many of his colleagues that the Protestant terrorist was distinctly less intelligent than his Catholic counterpart; well, bordering on stupid actually. This was confirmed many times over from the regular interviews he had conducted at Castlereagh Holding Centre, a unit that dealt solely with terrorist arrests and interviews.

Peter remembered his first weeks at North Queen Street C.I.D. offices. Early shift started at eight a.m., and as the 'new kid' on the block Peter always tried to be first into the office. The earlier start also meant Peter didn't have to sit in the busy morning traffic leading into Belfast. Try as he might he was never in the office before Bob Cook. He was part of C.I.D. folklore, and in an odd twist of fate, Peter later began a relationship with his daughter, unaware upon meeting her that she was in any way related, lest he may not have continued with the courtship ritual.

Bob was in his late fifties and had completed more police service than anyone else in the station. He hung on only because he was frightened of what he would do without the routine that he had. Bob was a member of his local bowling club, virtually a short jack's length from his house, but only because this was his closest bar, and the staff were flexible in applying licensing hours. Bob had only ever once stepped onto the hallowed bowling green lawn, and that had been entirely unintentional, and disastrous. He had been so pissed one night that the bar steward had refused to serve him any more drink – an action almost as unexpected as Bob subsequently stepping onto the revered lawn.

'Fuck you cunto,' was as much as Bob could conjure up at the time of his being refused more drink, and even he realised at the time that it didn't really deserve or invite a response.

'Right, give me a half bottle of Bush for a carryout,' slurred Bob, glad that he had not offended the bar steward.

The steward placed a half bottle of Bushmills whiskey on the bar and turned towards the till to ring in the amount payable. As he did so, Bob swiped the bottle from the bar top and staggered mistakenly towards the sliding glass doors that lead to the bowling green, rather than the exit door to the car park. He lived only a stones throw away, but most of the time as he was too drunk to walk he would rely on the car.

'Put it on the tab you fucking son of Killjoy,' Bob shouted, his left arm raised in the air in salute as his right hand tucked the bottle into the waistband of his trousers.

He managed to manoeuvre the slide doors open with only the slightest of effort, which left him amazed at his own skills. He looked back to admire his handiwork, now confused as to exactly where he was, and this was the mistake that in circumspect lead to the next chain of unfortunate events. As he slowly turned his head round in the direction he was staggering, his already forward momentum had taken him to the concrete balustrade about three feet above the lawn surface. As he tumbled over the balustrade, arms and hands instinctively outstretched to cushion his landing, he briefly imagined a cushioned touchdown provided by the manicured lawn surface. He had failed to take into account the gravel surface that lay between the balustrade and the immaculate bowling green, and struck the hardcore in a manner that many of those watching from within the safe confines of the Club House considered one of the best 'belly flops' they had ever witnessed.

As Bob lay prostrate and dazed, he felt a wet sensation affecting his upper legs, and said to himself as he reached his hands down to carry out a cursory examination, 'Fuck I hope that is blood.' In the darkness he was unable to see, so relied upon whatever his hands would reveal. He licked his hands as he stood up, hoping to sample the taste of his own blood. His devastation when his taste buds confirmed the presence of Bushmills whiskey would rank as probably one of the most disappointing moments in his life. The effect of this discovery caused him to stumble forward in shock, causing him to take his first, (and last), step onto the pristine bowling surface, where he took down his trousers and threw what remaining shards of the Bushmills whiskey bottle he could find across the esteemed members bowling lawn, fearful of ripping his testicles to pieces. He then sat down on the lawn and ran his hands up his legs in an attempt to recover whatever residue of whisky remained, sucking each hand greedily, but without any significant result.

Bob chose not to attend the subsequently convened disciplinary Bowling Club Committee Meeting hearing, and readily accepted his six month ban when notified in writing. The Chairman, himself a retired Police Officer, had worked tirelessly in his defence of Bob, and had allowed fiction to fudge reality when he claimed Bob was suffering from post-traumatic stress disorder. He also championed Bob's role as secretary of the P.S.N.I. Northern Ireland Football Supporters Club.

Bob was always sitting at his desk, a mug already in hand whenever Peter arrived at the C.I.D. office. Peter would prepare tea and coffee for the other Detectives he knew would arrive in the next half hour. On one particular morning Bob had left the office, and Peter thought he would take the opportunity to refill Bob's mug before he returned. Peter picked up the mug and found that it was still almost half full with what appeared to be green tea. He instinctively sniffed the contents and took a step back as the shocking aroma of cheap whisky assailed his senses. Peter was no slouch himself when it came to drinking, and he had on numerous occasions resorted to early morning drink 'cures,' but never at work. What was he to do with this scenario? He could report Bob to his superiors for disciplinary action, he could have a private word with Bob – unlikely because he had seldom more than grunted at Peter's presence, or he could, as he did, simply return the mug and say nothing.

Peter settled well into C.I.D. work and quickly became an accepted member of the North Queen Street Office. He seldom worked an eight hour day, ten to fourteen hours being the norm. The work excited him and rewarded him both financially and professionally, and this served to mask the detrimental effect it was having on his relationship with his wife and daughter before their untimely deaths. Although he worshipped them both it was difficult for them to appreciate what he had unknowingly committed himself to. It was not a superhuman cause for truth and justice; it was not a campaign against criminals and a fight for the victims. He simply and unexplainably found himself wrapped up in a community of likeminded Detectives who worked hard and partied even harder, though some like Bob were encouraged to forgo the former and assume an office coordination type of role. He ensured the stress cupboard was fully stocked at all times, calculating and issuing monthly bar bills, the relentless pursuit of settlement of monthly bar bills, and importantly for all concerned the manipulation of crime statistics in order to drastically increase office crime clearances. His other informal duties included telling bare faced lies over the phone to wives (and his daughter) enquiring of their Detective husband's whereabouts, acting as mediator during serious marital disputes, and the sale and supply of contraband goods brought into Ireland by his good mate Dick the lorry driver from the bowling club.

Peter enjoyed the morning routine as everyone gathered in what appeared to outsiders to be the C.I.D. filing room. This room housed all that was forbidden within Royal Ulster Constabulary police stations; the stress cupboard, colour television and satellite receiver, fake weapons (for various uses), excess ammunition obtained from range firing days, two camp beds, two summer duvets, spare suits and shirts in three sizes, and wash bags, to mention but a few. This was a self-sufficiency capsule that NASA would be proud of.

Everyone quickly gathered there with their tea, coffee and whiskey, and so the banter began. Only the occurrence of a serious terrorist incident would disrupt this routine, and the expediency of the response displayed relied less upon the nature of the incident, but more importantly the subject matter being bandied in the filing room.

Bob in particular liked to regale all present with historic tales of his early C.I.D. days, and he rarely let the truth get in the way of a good story. Bob became the central figure in each of his recounted scenes, even though many present knew that Bob had not been remotely involved. Bob's satanic gaze when fixed upon you, and his strategic seating position, caused many working Detectives to spend far too much time in early morning reverie. At times it took a superhuman struggle to extricate oneself from the morning worship. Peter still thought it a valuable contribution in helping to combat the daily misery that most Detectives encountered in their working day, the separation of fact from fiction that seemed to enable them to deal more objectively with incidents that otherwise may have caused them to adopt a personal emotional attachment.

'Well, that was very sensible for me,' Peter muttered to himself as he struggled from his bed into an upright position. He suddenly felt the need to steady himself by reaching out an arm against the wall in front of him. Maybe wasn't that sensible after all, but it was early in the morning and there was plenty of time for his body to recover before heading to the golf club.

He went into the kitchen to put the kettle on before opening the living room curtains. He glanced outside to make sure his car was parked correctly, and not appearing as if it had been abandoned by car thieves at the culmination of a high speed pursuit by police. The efficiency of his parking served to confirm that the quick visit to the golf club, despite the juniper berry crop failure, had not been over indulgent, but sensible indeed. He never for a moment considered why he needed to check his car's positioning. This was the thing that caused most friction between Peter and his girlfriend Anne, and as he checked his mobile phone he saw a late night text message from her urging him to leave the car at the golf club if he was going to have a few drinks. His failure to respond would be interpreted by Anne as proof that he had driven his car home after drinking too much. Peter knew Anne was a late riser so seized the initiative and sent a text message to her stating that he had only popped in for one drink, but accidentally left his phone in the car when he arrived home. He hoped it would be enough to prevent any discussion on the subject. He also knew Anne was the daughter of Bob Cook, and had experienced through her mother the myriad excuses and smoke screens police detectives were capable of manufacturing.

It was six thirty and Peter was teeing off at eight a.m. He knew that Spit in the Chips, Necro and Wing, the other members of his four ball, would be at the golf club for a beer before teeing off. Anne was coming to Whitehead for the day, meeting at the golf club for lunch around one p.m. As Peter readied himself he took the decision to forego the early morning beer, telling himself that his coordination was often out of synch even when sober. Meeting at around one p.m. for lunch generally meant Anne would arrive nearer to two p.m., so Peter knew he had plenty of time for a drink after the golf, and before Anne's arrival.

CHAPTER THREE – A NEW SUB DIVISIONAL COMMANDER

Brett Mayne was the uniformed Superintendent, Sub Divisional Commander, for Newtownabbey. Newtownabbey was a Sub Division of D Division which covered most of North Belfast. Brett Mayne's Sub Division as he liked to call it also included Carrickfergus Police Station, and in particular C Section, that was Brett's personal nemesis, and several outlying country villages. Newtownabbey itself was a densely populated area, consisting mainly of protestant Housing Authority estates, one of which, Rathcoole, was considered the largest in Northern Ireland at its construction. It was a grim, forbidding place for the majority of decent law abiding residents, who lived their daily lives in an environment of fear and intimidation from the loyalist paramilitaries who ran the estate. As so often in Northern Ireland, 'paramilitaries' was a euphemism for the criminal gangs that peddled drugs, sold illicit alcohol and cigarettes, carried out random punishment beatings, and demanded protection money from the small cash strapped businesses supplying the local community.

Brett had been in charge for only two weeks, his first operational deployment since his probation period, and he longed for a return to the demanding environment of Headquarters policing. As so often with officers with a long career in Headquarters policing, 'demanding' was a euphemism for cosseted and removed from reality.

Brett was in his early thirties and had joined the Police Service of Northern Ireland after completing his PhD in Soviet Hieroglyphics at the University of Manchester. He was almost five feet and four inches in height, and had chosen the Accelerated Promotion scheme offered by the Police Service of Northern Ireland, as the new Force had decided to eliminate minimum height criteria as part of their overall anti-discrimination policy. Brett spoke with a slight, but noticeable stutter, and abhorred physical confrontation.

Brett was tactless, a poor communicator, and lacked 'people skills' – three of the most important qualities the public would expect of a police officer. Psychological interviews, role playing scenarios and character assessments, conducted during Brett's recruitment process failed to highlight these glaring deficiencies.

The Police Service of Northern Ireland received their first complaint about Brett's conduct when he was a probationary officer in Larne on foot patrol in the town centre for his very first time. The Main Street in Larne is only slightly more charming than that of Carrickfergus. The distance between the two towns is only fifteen miles, but worlds apart in terms of local character. Larne residents tended to shuffle about the Main Street in a zombie like 'Living Dead' fashion, wearing incestuous grins on their faces. Fashion shops appeared to be excluded from the town. Quite simply there was no need.

Brett had detected a Suzuki Vitara jeep parked in a bus bay outside the post office on Main Street. He stood by the vehicle, tutted in utter dismay at the effrontery of the missing driver, and removed the Fixed Penalty Notice book from his pocket. 'Some people eh,' he stuttered to himself as he added the vehicle details to the carbon forms, looking around him at the passing public, waiting for their adulation, or at the very least their nods of approval, as if he had just put to the sword several slaves in gladiatorial combat in a packed coliseum.

'Constable, it's mine,' shouted the heavily pregnant woman as she tried to negotiate the steps from the Post Office onto Main Street.

'I am eight months pregnant; I only parked there for a few minutes to cash the family allowance.'

'Doubtless you will be looking forward to an increase in be, be, benefits soon then Madam,' replied Brett without any hint of humour or understanding.

'Constable, please don't give me a ticket, I won't park there again. Lesson learned.'

'Lady, take a loo, loo, look at the rear of your vehicle.'

'It's in a bus bay, it's not a hanging offence.'

'Your tow, tow, tow bar is ob, obscuring the rear number plate, in contravention of con, construction and use regulations, and that is serious.'

Brett went on to detail that if her car was to be used in a murder, robbery or fatal accident that potential witness evidence would be lost by not being able to read the rear number plate.

'We got the car from the dealer like this; I didn't know there was anything wrong. Please Constable, I don't want a fine, I will get it fixed as soon as I can.'

'I am letting you off, off with the parking. If I let you off with this it could be the star, star, start of a criminal career. Offenders need to be pun, punished.'

The heavily pregnant woman started to cry and attracted the support from the public that Brett had craved only minutes earlier. He did complete and apply the Fixed Penalty Notice for allowing the vehicle tow bar to obscure the rear number plate. He wisely decided to attach it to the offending vehicle rather than hand it to the pregnant driver who was on her back on the pavement screaming in pain, being attended to by increasing numbers of the passing public, several of whom had flagged down a passing ambulance.

The ensuing complaints about Brett's conduct, and threat of civil litigation against the Police Service of Northern Ireland whenever in contact with the public, served to propel him towards an office career far sooner than he had anticipated. This was an unexpected bonus for Brett, and an incalculable relief for the general public.

Brett considered himself to be part of the cutting edge of New Age policing. His reputation was not going to be made by heroic tales of derring do, or sleuth like investigative prowess; Brett saw his future in the efficient gathering and analysis of Crime and Traffic statistics, Force Mission Statements, Ethics and Moral Codes of Practice, Business and Service Improvement, Police Discipline Code, and the other ancillary minutiae that he considered to be the vital cogs in the wheel that drives any modern Police Force.

It was as a result of his first visit to Carrickfergus Police Station, and C Section personnel then on duty, that Brett labelled it lawless, and made it his personal crusade to rid it of the former Royal Ulster Constabulary deadwood that had contributed to its falling below the standards required of the Police Service of Northern Ireland. He had not long been appointed Sub Divisional Commander, and decided to call in unannounced, in his own car, and in civilian clothes, to Carrickfergus Police Station.

It was seven thirty a.m. and C Section were on early duty. As he stopped his car at the security barrier entrance there was no sign of the Reserve Constable on duty. He waited for the officer to emerge from the security room adjacent to the barrier, and when he failed to do so Brett sounded his car horn. Reserve Constable Tony Stockman would later recount that this was not a simple touch of the car horn intended to attract attention, but a long aggressive sounding of the car horn with hostile intent.

Tony half stumbled from the security room, annoyed at being woken abruptly from his post breakfast nap. He wore no uniform hat, his shirt collar was open, and his tie clipped onto his shirt pocket. With his hands in his pockets he walked the few steps towards the driver's door of the offending vehicle as slowly as he could.

'There is a cemetery behind this station, are you trying to wake the bloody dead,' said Tony, as he summed up the diminutive figure in a suit through the open drivers door window. Ron the Station Duty Officer had left the front desk because of the din and walked towards the entrance barrier.

'Co, Co, Constable, do you, know, know, know, who I am,' Brett responded, shocked at the sloppy appearance, and attitude, of the Reserve Constable at his driver's door.

Tony saw Ronny approaching and called out to him, 'Ronny, for fuck sake call a Doctor we have a stuttering dwarf here who doesn't know who he is.'

Ronny decided to take charge of the situation and leaned into the car window, 'Sir, this is a police station. What I suggest you do is rejoin the main road and drive citywards....,' but before Ronny could obligingly provide directions to the nearest hospital he was stopped very abruptly mid sentence by Brett. 'I am Superintendent May, May, Mayne, your Sub Divisional Co, Co, Co, Commander.'

'Warrant Card please sir,' Tony requested with some authority.

Brett produced his warrant card for inspection by Tony, who then handed it to Ronny as if verification was required.

'Ah, so you knew all along,' said Tony, hoping that an injection of mild humour might assist in damage limitation.

'I need to see, see, see, your Sergeant immediately,' Brett demanded.

'No problems, now that we all know who you are just you go ahead, I am sure she is free at the moment and will be delighted to meet you.'

Ronny by this stage had sped towards Sergeant Reid's office in order to give her some warning of the stuttering dwarfs impending arrival.

Alison Reid had unzipped her uniform trousers to mitigate the effect of the large breakfast she had just consumed, and was lying across two chairs pushed together to form as close to a bed as she could muster. Ronny's abrupt entrance had disturbed her from her post breakfast reverie, as Brett Mayne had done to Tony some minutes earlier.

'Ali, the SDC is on his way, he looks like Napoleon with a stutter, and is a tad unhappy.'

'Why, oh bloody why. Has he nothing better to do at seven thirty in the morning. Thanks Ronny.'

Alison stood up and looked into the mirror in the Sergeant's office. She truly was at her dishevelled best. She tried to push her unwashed hair into a tight bun but it fell flat around her shoulders. She was free of makeup and wearing the same white uniform shirt from the day before. The heavy creases looked like permanent fixtures, as if they were a part of the shirt, and incapable of removal by the most fervent ironing. She checked the underarms and saw the brown discolouration caused by excessive sweating and a dearth of deodorant.

'I look like shit,' she had the courage to say to herself, just as Brett Mayne entered the Sergeant's office.

'And you, you, are, are, are, who exactly.'

'I will answer that when you tell me who you are exactly,' said Alison, amazed at Ronny's brief but uncanny description of the very perplexed stuttering dwarf in a suit now standing in front of her.

'I am Superintendent May, May, May, Mayne, the new Sub Divisional Commander.'

'I am Sergeant Alison Reid, C Section.'

There was no attempt at a handshake by either party.

'From what little I have see, see, seen, this Section is a dis, disgrace, and that includes you, you Sergeant.'

If he was referring to personal appearances Sergeant Reid was not in a position to defend herself.

'Appearances can be deceptive Sir; I have a good Section here.'

'Appearances are ev, ev, everything Sergeant. No ties, no uniform cap, col, collar open, and sleeves roll, rolled up. More like builders lab, lab, lab.'

'Labourers Sir, I think I get your point.'

'Get this Section sorted Sergeant, I don't like your atti, atti, attit.'

'Attitude Sir.'

'Ex, exactly what I mean. You may be ex RUC and stu, stuck in your RUC ways, we are now a modern force with modern val, values. I am watching this Section very closely from now, now, now on.'

'We strive to improve in every way Sir, and valued professional criticism from a Senior Officer of your undoubted experience is always welcomed. It will allow me to set a benchmark for improvement that will enable C Section to attain the exacting standards demanded of the PSNI.'

'Maybe I underestimated that Sergeant,' Brett thought to himself, as he walked towards the car park.

'Fucking new age wanker,' Sergeant Reid thought to herself before Brett had reached the door from the Sergeant's office.

Brett's appraisal of C Section, Carrickfergus, had improved slightly after hearing the very conciliatory but professional approach adopted by Sergeant Reid. For a man who believed that the metaphor of never judge a book by its cover was misguided nonsense, he had dismissed Sergeant Reid's appearance as a minor aberration, concentrating instead on her positive approach to continuous improvement. This was further evidence of his distinct lack of people skills.

On arrival at Newtownabbey Police Station the Reserve Constable at the entrance barrier came smartly to attention and Brett nodded in approval. After parking his car in the Sub Divisional Commanders bay he walked through the Enquiry Office and the Station Duty Officer, a Constable whose name Brett felt he had no need to remember, also came smartly to attention. Brett chose not to acknowledge this deference. Bloody smart though, and exactly what he thought Sergeant Reid would inculcate into the rebel members of C Section, Carrickfergus.

Brett walked into his office and could still detect the odour of freshly applied paint. He had used a considerable chunk of his Sub Divisional Commanders social fund to ensure that his office befitted someone of his rank and self-importance. The previous incumbent had served almost thirty years with the Royal Ulster Constabulary, and despite this was still held in high regard with police officers, local dignitaries and low life's alike. Brett's first task on assuming office was to get rid of the beer fridge and globe of the world on castors that contained every imaginable alcoholic spirit. He also insisted on the removal of the wall mounted television and satellite receiver that was encoded to display all sports generally, but horse racing specifically. The generous oak bookcase that once contained beer, wine, whisky and brandy glasses now accommodated the latest in judicial reviews, Butterworths, new law journals and the latest in Sweet & Maxwell publications, none of which Brett had read.

This morning was to be spent in administering verbal warnings to errant police officers who had committed wrongdoings that did not amount to immediate disciplinary procedures or investigation by the Internal Investigations Team, or Police Ombudsman's Office. Sometimes these warnings would be the first in a process that would ultimately lead to a police officer's dismissal. This was not the confrontational type of meeting which Brett was enthusiastic to avoid. Brett enjoyed with a little more than smug satisfaction at being able to assert his power over the career fearing non-confrontational souls who sat in front of him.

Brett had his desk and chair mounted on a thick perspex base, covered in carpet, that allowed him to appear to be at the very least at the same height as those in front of him. Occasionally he appeared to be inches taller, and this delighted him. Pride of place on his desk was two framed photographs of his wife Angel and three year old son Robert Peel Mayne. Angel was a former policewoman who saw in Brett a means to ensure a rapid end to a working life that she was not suited to. A more detailed analysis would conclude that Angel was not suited to any form of working life. Her feelings for Brett ranged from ambivalent at best, to hatred, but marriage to Brett provided a pathway to the 'do nothing' lifestyle she so craved. The knowledge very soon into the marriage that Brett was demanding of a child to complete the family unit shocked Angel. She had lost her virginity to Brett on her honeymoon night at the age of 28. That she had remained 'virgo intacta' for so long was not due to an adherence to a virtuous lifestyle, but rather that she was wholly unattracted to men, and genetically indisposed to sexual arousal in any form. She endured sexual intercourse on her wedding night with the same enthusiasm that a torture victim embraces having electrodes attached to their genitals. To repeat the Neanderthal process until conception was almost too high a price to pay. Only Brett's promise to employ a live-in nanny, and never show any signs of sexual behaviour post conception, convinced her to have the brat. The absence of any feelings of sexual arousal was soon surpassed by Angels lack of maternal love. Angel disliked Robert Peel Mayne almost as much as she did his father.

He looked very briefly through the six discipline files that lay in his in tray, all very boring mundane stuff that seemed to offer no opportunity for Brett to verbally assail the transgressors into tearful pleas for leniency. He threw the files back into his in tray while he waited on his morning coffee being brought by one of the administration office staff, and was suddenly struck by the recognition of the name displayed on the top most file. He retrieved the file of Constable Ronald Cutler. This was the Station Duty Officer from Carrickfergus C Section who had tried to give him directions to a hospital earlier that morning, tie less, and lacking in respect. Brett started to read Constable Cutler's file in detail.

Cutler was 45 years of age, and Brett was very surprised to read that he joined the Royal Ulster Constabulary after completing a degree in Biblical Hebrew. He was less surprised to read that Cutler eschewed all attempts to have him embark on the Accelerated Promotion Scheme for graduates on the grounds that he had no interest in personal development, and wished to progress his career by doing as little as possible. Brett paused, a sick feeling welling in his stomach, disgusted not by Cutler's apathy, but the thought that he could possibly have reached the same lofty rank as himself, and the dire consequences that would have had for the Police Service of Northern Ireland. Brett read on; Cutler had been restricted to station duties for most of his service on the recommendations of Force Medical

Officers and eminent psychiatrists. 'Damned ridiculous,' Brett thought. Whilst it was okay

for Brett to be sheltered from dealing with the hordes of the great unwashed as he liked to

refer to the less well educated general public, he felt Cutler had no such right. Police officers

in Northern Ireland were exposing themselves to the risk of terrorist attack on a daily basis

on the streets of Northern Ireland, and Cutler should not be hiding within the safe haven

walls of the police station. Brett of course knew that he was destined for higher things, via a

very different police career path that did not involve interaction with the public. Cutler's latest

adverse report, a computer generated report, outlined his consistent and excessive absence

from work due to sickness. It was Brett's task to find out from Cutler the reason for these

absences, and hopefully administer a verbal warning as a first step in removing him from his

police force. Cutler had got away with things for too long, and had no place in Brett's Police

Service. Cutler was first on his list and due in his office at 10 a.m. – just enough time to

drink his coffee, close his eyes, and recall the feeling of his son's nanny's lingerie slipping

through his fingers when he delved through her passionately scented knicker drawer some

hours earlier whilst she attended to Robert Peel Mayne. He had been careful all morning

since then to avoid washing or contaminating his left hand in any way lest the scent

disappear. It had been absolutely necessary to wash his right hand after wiping clean some

areas of lingerie before returning them to the drawer.

At 10.15 a.m. Brett's reverie was disturbed by a knock on his office door. Slightly startled

and lost in thought, he looked up at the clock in his office as Constable Cutler entered

uninvited.'

Co, Constable Cutler, you are 15 minutes late'

'Sir, first of all if you please, I do not stand on rank, I am not consumed by it, in fact I think

very little of any rank and class structured society, so please call me Ronnie.'

Brett was stunned into silence, his brain struggling to come to terms with this affront. Ronnie by now had settled into the faux leather chair in front of Brett's desk, and he could see that Ronnie had made no attempt to smarten his appearance for this meeting with a very superior officer. He wore no uniform cap, and his hair resembled an unkempt and overgrown adolescent Michael Jackson wig. His moustache was of a type that was popular with porn stars of the 1970s. Brett was at a loss where to start, but had to regain the initiative, and more importantly the moral standing of someone as important as he considered himself. He also made a mental note to consult the Police Codes and Regulations regarding the permitted maximum length for the growth of moustaches.

'Ron, Ron, Constable, yes Con Constable Cutler, you are 15 minutes late – explain'

'Sir, I know that a senior officer like you did not achieve high office by sticking to rigid punctuality. The flow way is your way, and that's what makes you stand out from the rest'

I didn't te, tell you to sit dow, down'

'No sir, but knowing how valuable your time is I did so without you having to ask''

Brett realised it was best to keep this meeting short and bring it to a conclusion as soon as possible.

'Now Constable Cu, Cutler, it is my duty today to elucidate from you the rea, reason for your prolonged and frank, frankly ridiculous level of absence from work due to sick, sickness'

'Sir, before I continue, I would like to congratulate you on your command of the English language. A truly forgotten art form, you should consider yourself a master of the craft if you don't mind me saying so'

Brett found his voice raising uncontrollably as he dug the gold tipped nib of his Mont Blanc fountain pen into the outer folder of Constable Cutler's Personal File , 'Just ex, explain to me the rea, reason…'

'Well Sir, I am attempting to do just that, but for your interruptions if you don't mind me saying so'

Brett felt his brain enlarge inside his skull, his face was crimson, and sweat soaked his shirt collar and trickled down his back. His mouth was dry and he struggled to find the moisture to enable him to speak.

'Just plea, please let's get this o, over with. Simply tell me wh, why you'

'Of course Sir, that's why I am here,' Ronnie interrupted. 'Someone as well read as you is doubtless familiar with the works, or some may say work,' of Joseph Heller, and in particular Catch 22'

Ronnie paused for response but saw only a bemused and startled figure in front of him so he continued.

'I have Sir, a condition which I refer to as Yossarianism. A slightly different symptom to that manifested by the central character of Catch 22 of which my disease is eponymous'

'What on this gods ea, earth are you on about. You are si, sick more often than you ap, appear for duty with an ill, illness that you have con, concocted from a book'

Ronnie stood up and picked up one of the framed photographs from Brett's desk.

'Sir, what wonderful photographs you have on your desk. These are undoubtedly your wife and son. What beautiful people they are, you are a very lucky man and must be so proud…

Before Ronnie could finish, Brett was on his feet, disappointed that he was still short of Ronnie's height, 'Get out Cu, Cutler, get out of my office now. Go, go' he shouted, pointing towards the door.

The last words Brett heard as Ronnie departed were Constable Cutler's reminder that he should call him Ronnie. As Ronnie departed, deliberately failing to close the office door, Brett felt a wet sensation on his right thigh and looked down to see that the ink that had drained from his Mont Blanc fountain pen via the broken nib had permeated the fabric of his

Armani suit trousers. He would later discover the ink impossibly difficult to scrub from his

thigh. He found a biro and wrote upon Ronnie's file, 'verbal warning administered.'

CHAPTER FOUR – A GRUESOME DISCOVERY

Ronnie had taken Sergeant Reid's unmarked, armoured, Ford Escort supervision vehicle to drive from Carrickfergus for his meeting with Superintendent Mayne. This vehicle from a distance would not attract undue attention. Only when close up would the untrained eye be able to detect the opaque reflection from the armoured windows and windscreen; windows that for obvious reasons remained sealed closed. During infrequent hot spells the inadequate air conditioning tended to create a mini weather system of its own within the confines of the vehicle due to the amount of water that leaked from the internal unit onto the fixtures and fittings, combining with oppressive hear during summer months. The speed of the vehicle was also seriously impaired by the weight of the B6 armour fitted inside and underneath the vehicle.

The vehicle was sparklingly clean inside after being recently returned to duty use. Some weeks previously someone had secreted a bag containing meat pasties and butchers tripe under the passenger seat of the vehicle. As the days passed, supervisors using the vehicle commented on an unpleasant smell when they completed the vehicle log books at the end of their duties. As the weeks passed, what had originally been reported as an unpleasant smell had developed into a foul, putrid stench, and supervisors avoided using the vehicle altogether. Most supervisors were content not to remove themselves from the police station, whilst others simply had patrol vehicles collect them when needed.

The Motor Transport officer, a Reserve Constable with no qualifications or experience in mechanical engineering, had been selected for the post because his obesity made it nigh on impossible for the Force Tailors to expand upon the basic police issue tunic, shirt, and trousers in order to accommodate his bulk. He was in charge of a civilian assistant/driver, though he did not allow this power of authority to influence him in any way. Both men, boss and serf, were chain smokers, in an office and work area that emanated a film like vapour of petroleum spirit. Health and safety warning notices of naked flames, inflammable materials, and hazardous chemicals, had been obscured by an accumulation of nicotine on the surfaces as a result of continuous cigarette smoking. Ben and Joe, boss and serf respectively, had few visitors to their offices, except for police officers who could not be bothered to attend the designated smoking area in the station complex. Both were annoyed however when reading the comments in the vehicle log book about the foul aroma inside the Ford Escort. Ben prided himself on Joe's efforts at vehicle cleaning, and both interpreted the comments as an insult to Joe's professionalism. In truth, when Ben was in the station canteen, bereft of Joe's company, he would openly imply to all those with a vested interest, or indeed anyone at all, that in his opinion as a boss/supervisor Joe's standards had been slipping. Ben decided it was time for management involvement in order to solve the problem with the Ford Escort, and told Joe he would assist him in another, more thorough cleaning of the car. It had been wrongly assumed that the smell was caused by discarded carry out food, milk, or other noxious liquid/food that had permeated the fabric of the seats or interior flooring.

Ben and Joe were sitting in their very small smoke filled office, drinking tea from oil stained mugs, whilst attempting to draw nicotine into their lungs from counterfeit cigarettes that had been mass produced in a child labour factory in China. To the discerning smoker the taste was akin to smoking rolled up cardboard. To Ben and Joe they represented great value for money, and the implication that they may be illegal was never considered. After all, Ben bought them from Bob a trustworthy Detective at North Queen Street, who got them from a friend, so no further legitimacy was required.

'Joe, when we are done, bring the Escort round to the wash bay while I get the steam cleaner sorted out''

'You don't have experience in the steam cleaner department Ben, maybe better you bring the car round'

'It's only a fucking steam cleaner, should I be NASA qualified or some fucking thing'

Ben loved the word fuck, and all its derivatives, and tended to include it in each sentence, most commonly in its noun or adjective form.

'Just thinking health and safety Ben, you know what we're up against here. Shouldn't you be doing a risk assessment before we even start this'

'What the fuck are you on about. Risk, only fucking risk is that you will have to work harder. Start all that shit and before you know it there's no fucking smoking here. I am making the decision Joe, that's what comes with being senior management'

'Let's just have another quick cig before we start'

'Good idea Joe, there's fucking management potential in you mate''

Cigarettes over, Joe walked over to the Ford Escort, knowing that the keys would have been left in the ignition. The car had been unmoved, indeed unopened, for two days, two particularly warm and sunny days. The effect of the sun and heat on the armoured glass caused the interior to become an oven on wheels. A number of police officers had been shot over the years simply because they left armoured vehicle doors open when static in order to breathe cool, fresh air. Joe, without considering the effects, opened the driver door and slid immediately into the driver seat. The weight of the reinforced armoured door caused it to slam shut just before it crushed Joe's trailing leg. A lifetime of smoking had most certainly diminished Joe's sense of smell, but nothing could disguise or prevent the inhalation of the disgusting, putrid smell caused by the rotten meat and tripe, being devoured by maggots. The larva that had reached adulthood now inhabited the vehicle interior, feasting greedily on the rotten mass at will. Joe was unconscious pretty much as the driver door crashed shut behind him.

After waiting 15 minutes and having another cigarette, Ben went in search of Joe. He went to the canteen, a venue where he would normally find Joe at any time of the day, and who's standard response upon being discovered was, 'Just passing through.' Joe would normally be found during off peak periods in the canteen seated with May the canteen assistant, and which ever cook was working Carrickfergus that day. It was rumoured that something was going on between Joe and May, but even Ben's physical abundance found it impossible to digest the harsh reality of such a liaison.

The canteen was empty save for May the canteen assistant sitting at one of the cracked formica tables, drinking tea. With her spare hand she was scratching her initials into the exposed wooden surface area of the table, with a knife removed from a plate left untouched since breakfast service some hours earlier.

'Hi May, you seen Joe'

'Not on duty, it's my tea break'

'Not asking you to fucking sauté him, just asking if you have seen him in the last 20 minutes'

'No I haven't, must be hard for you keeping a track on all your staff, maybe you need a P.A. or an assistant'

'Fucking funny for you May, but no fucking help. If he comes in tell him to get back to the office'

'Fuck off'

'Did you miss the compass catering lesson on fucking etiquette and customer care?'

'Fuck off Sir'

Ben stormed out of the canteen, well in fact he shuffled as quickly as someone of his obscene bulk would permit, determined to put into practice the adage that if you want a job done well, do it yourself, suspecting that Joe had adapted and put into practice the adage that you should never do today what you can put off until tomorrow. It was of slight concern to Ben that Joe was missing in action.

Ben approached the armoured Ford Escort, lacking the determination now to carry out the thorough cleaning job on his own, but certainly clear in his mind that he would drive the vehicle to the wash bay in preparation for the work to be done, smoke a cigarette, and await Joe's return from his period of Absence Without Leave. Ben opened the driver door of the supervision car and the waft of cooked and decaying flesh wrapped itself around his body, and caused him to step back from the car in a movement recorded as possibly one of his fastest in recent memory. As he stepped back Joe fell from the driver seat onto the gravel road surface, gasping for air like a goldfish out of water.

'Fuck sake Joe, what are you doing napping in that fucking car, its stinking'

'Napping' said Joe, struggling for breath, struggling to his feet, and searching desperately for his cigarettes, 'Napping you say, I nearly bloody died you dick, there is something dead in that car or Saddam has dumped some killing agent in it'

Ben helped Joe to his feet and placed a cigarette in his trembling hands.

'Bloody strong right enough, nearly fucking knocked me over and it would take a Hiroshima powered blast wave to fucking do that.' Ben tried to defuse the situation and calm Joe down with an injection of humour. 'Ha, apparently it was recorded as a very nice August day in Hiroshima before the bomb fell.' Joe was still unsteady on his feet, his eyes glazed.

Ben felt a surge of guilt and very gingerly opened up both the driver and passenger door of the car to allow a flow of fresh air to pass through.

'Back to the office for a brew and a cig then we will sort this fucking car out Joe'

'I might need the hospital Ben,' Joe spluttered in between alternate gasps of his cigarette and fresh air.

'We don't need any trouble Joe, brew and a cig and you will be fine.'

As they both relaxed and recovered in the office, conversation was put on hold while the mug of hot tea and cigarette were allowed to begin to speed up the recuperative process. Ben considered that if he were in fact to report the incident to his authorities it would surely mean that he might be considered for a bravery or lifesaving award. He would for the rest of his life, believe that he had saved Joe from a premature end to his. Furthermore he would recount his life saving antics with increasing embellishments for the rest of his life.

'Joe, let's go, think of it like a fallen rider getting straight back onto the fucking horse, don't let it beat you'

'No way am I driving that car'

'Management decision, we check the car where it's parked to find out what is causing the fucking smell, and then take it from there. Fail to plan, plan to fail Joe, its managerial speak.'

The flies were still buzzing around inside the car despite both doors lying open. The stench was still evident upon approach but not nearly as bad. They started by opening the boot of the vehicle and slowly removing and cursorily examining each item; hazard warning triangles, police accident signs, scene tape, yellow police bollards, first aid kit, evidence bags, high visibility vests, empty wine bottles, and other ancillary pieces of equipment. The smell was barely detectable at the rear of the vehicle so they decided to move, rather warily, to examine the interior. Ben elected for the front passenger seat area and Joe the drivers.

With no small amount of effort Ben got onto his knees on the gravel surface outside of the passenger door, leaned his upper body into the foot well, and visibly examined the mat and carpet. At the same time as he ran his right hand over the surfaces, he used his left hand to swat off flies. The smell was beginning to overpower him, but the effort required for him to return to his feet and step back in order to breathe in some fresh air outweighed the beneficial effects he may have derived.

He tried to lever the passenger seat back in its position but it proved resistant. He pulled up his left shirt sleeve and manoeuvred his arm underneath the seat, when his fingers made contact with a gooey, lumpy substance. He pushed his fingers in even deeper, and then felt what he later discovered were the movements of the maggots across his fingers investigating the newly arrived very plump flesh digits. He wrenched his arm out, falling backwards, unintentionally grabbing a small handful of the putrid substance as he did so. His back struck the gravel, and he lay like an overturned and overweight turtle, unable to bring himself to an upright position without assistance. He looked quickly at the contents of his left hand, and screamed out in a fashion that would haunt Joe forever.

'Joe, Joe, get me up, it's fucking brain matter, and we have got a fucking murder here.'

Joe rushed round and helped Ben to his feet. He held his left arm aloft as if holding an Olympic torch before slowly bringing it down for closer examination. He could only glance at it before fighting the gag reflex that was surely going to make him vomit if he didn't remove it from his hand immediately. Joe had never seen brain matter before. It would become clear before the end of the day, that Ben had never actually seen brain matter either. Many operational officers later suggested that not only had they never seen brain matter before, they never actually possessed any.

'Quick Joe, round the back and get me one of the evidence bags to put this brain matter into. Swarfega, or bloody bleach, I need to scrub my hand, fucking disgusting'

As soon as this was done, Ben and Joe closed the doors of the vehicle and sealed off the immediate area using scene preservation tape. Back at Ben's office with the evidence bag containing the brain matter, Ben phoned Alison Reid the duty Sergeant and asked her to come to his office as soon as possible, it was urgent, but he could not say anything over the phone. Ben had known Alison for nearly 20 years, through good times and bad. Alison knew from Ben's voice that something was seriously amiss, and knew better than to try and question him over the phone.

Alison walked the few steps from the station building to Ben's office beside the car wash bay. She walked into the office, and despite the fog of cigarette smoke, she could see that both men were shaken, almost in a state of shock.

'Ali, the supervision car, the Escort, there is a dead body under the passenger seat' Ben blurted out. 'The bag here is full of fucking brain matter.' Alison looked at the contents, she unfortunately had seen brain matter on several occasions, and while she doubted the contents were in fact brain matter she knew she was not qualified to confirm or deny that.

'Well Ben, if it is a dead body, it is a very small body to fit underneath the passenger seat'

'Maybe it was only the head dumped there; you need to get C.I.D., Scenes of Crime, Forensic. The new Sub Divisional Commander needs to know'

'Whoa there Ben. Ray the S.O.C.O is in the building, I will get him to have a look before we set off the alarm buttons, no C.I.D., no telling anyone else until S.O.C.O. gives us a clearer indication. You and Joe remain here – tell no one.'

Alison collected the evidence bag and went to the main building to find Ray McGreevy, the Scenes of Crime Officer she saw going into the C.I.D. office some minutes prior to receiving Ben's panicked phone call. She was in luck, Ray had only called in to collect an exhibit for later examination, and was about to leave the building when Alison saw him.

Alison had known Ray for as long as she had known Ben. He too was old school. She knew Ray was an irascible character, and had earned the nickname 'Greenpeace' from Detectives who regarded him as something of an 'energy conservationist' when asked to attend and examine scenes in detail. Alison beckoned Ray into her office and outlined the background of the mystery smell in the supervision car, Ben's discovery, and then handed Ray the evidence bag containing the suspected brain matter. He looked inside the open investigation bag, even sniffed the contents, an action that would have caused Ben and Joe to faint had they been present.

'First of all, if it had been suspected evidence of an offence it would have been worthless as the bag is unsealed and therefore all integrity is lost. I am pretty certain I know what it is but will look under the seat anyway.'

Alison led Ray to the supervision vehicle, still sealed off in the parking area, and Ray opened his scene examination case. Instead of donning the disposable protective coat, hat and shoe coverings he would normally have done so at a crime scene, he simply pulled a pair of surgical gloves over his hands. He bent down under the front passenger seat and made a cursory examination of what remained. Minutes later he had finished, whispered in Alison's ear, removed his gloves and walked with her to Ben's office.

'Well Greenpeace, some major shit here' Ben stammered as they came through the door.

'Christ Ben you have put the weight on boy' Ray said, handing back the evidence bag.

'Fuck off Greenpeace.'

'I had a look underneath; there is still some of the crust there'

'Ah for fuck sake, the fucking skull, that's gross'

'No Ben, the crust, what you have there is the remains of a meat pastie, possibly accompanied by butcher's tripe, but I would need the Forensic Lab to confirm that.'

Ray and Ali burst out laughing. Ben and Joe looked at each other, Joe rather more accusingly, wondering why Ben had dragged him into this. As Ray and Ali left the office, Ray couldn't help a last dig at Ben.

'Don't be eating the rest of it Ben, its way past sell by date.'

They could only hear the disguised muffle of Ben shouting and swearing from behind the closed door.

And so it was that Ronnie found himself driving towards Carrickfergus police station in an armoured vehicle with an uncannily pristine interior, weighed down even more by the presence of innumerable air fresheners. As he drove along the marine highway he looked to his left and saw Des emerge from Bewleys café, one hand covering his crotch, the other dusting down the front of his coat, taking his first step towards the police station. Ronnie picked up the radio hand set, intending to pick him up and return him to the station.

'Delta 54 from Delta 50 send your location over'

Des panicked and hesitated, he recognised the Delta 50 call sign as being that of Sergeant Reid, and the voice as that of Ronnie Cutler, and knew that occasionally he would drive her around the area. He need time to compose himself before meeting with them.'

'Em, Delta 50 from Delta 54, em, outside the Joymount Arms off Marine Highway over'

Des was in fact several hundred yards from the Joymount Arms. Ronnie wondered why he was prevaricating, and decided to drive the unmarked vehicle and meet him. He was stopped at traffic lights outside of the library (a seldom used institution in Carrickfergus save for individuals sheltering from the rain – though it did hold the UK record for lowest number of late and non-returned books). Waiting for the light to change to green Ronnie heard a loud rumble emanate from his stomach, the effects of a particularly spicy curry, and too many cans of Guinness from the night before. He did not know whether to fart or not but nature took over and fart he did, uncontrollably. 'Oh fuck a follow through' shouted Ronnie to know one in particular. He quickly felt his trousers under the crotch area 'thank fuck,' dry.

Ronnie brought the supervision car slowly to a halt behind Des and pressed the police siren button. Des nearly jumped out of his uniform and Ronnie beckoned him to get into the passenger seat for a lift back to the station. Des eased into the passenger seat, and Ronnie sped off, causing him to fall back into the seat, and the door to crash shut, forming the air tight seal required of armoured vehicles.

'For god's sake Ronnie, you smelly arsed bollocks, what the fuck is that.'

'And exactly which genus of rose scent did you expect from my troubled anus'

Des put his hand over his mouth and nose and began to try and mutter through his closed lips, while trying to hold his breath at the same time. He managed about 30 seconds but was forced again to inhale. As he exhaled, vomit accompanied the exhalation, expertly directed between Des's legs onto the passenger foot well.

'Tut tut Oedipus, did you miss the syntax lesson at the Training Centre. This is so not the right time or place for showing off your projectile vomit skills.' And so it was Des spent the time before lunch cleaning the passenger foot well for the second time in a very short period, and more often that Ben and Joe had done in a year prior to the meat pastie incident. Des had plenty of available room in his stomach to accommodate his lunch.

CHAPTER FIVE – SATURDAY MORNING GOLF GOES AWRY

It was a beautiful morning when Peter arrived at the Golf Club car park at around 7.30 a.m., and it was already nearly a quarter full. He went into the bar to find Spit in the Chips and Wing already standing at the bar drinking pints of Guinness, four hours before legal opening time. They were accompanied by several others, golfers and non-golfers, standing shoulder to shoulder, warriors in a small victorious army indulging in early morning, illegal imbibing. Some of the regular non-golfers had left their dogs tied to railings near to the main entrance doors, their wives pondering why dog and master were both piling on weight despite the time away from home devoted to exercise. Peter's early resolve crumbled before even reaching the bar when he agreed to a pint of Guinness when offered by Wing. The full time steward commenced the skilful process of pouring Peter's pint. His nickname was 'Turpin' as it was suspected by some, and known by many, that he observed the conduct, nay privilege of many bar stewards in order to supplement his meagre income, of every possible kind of small and thinly disguised deception.

'Thanks Turpin, cheers boys, where is Wardrobe'

'Still pissed so he isn't fucking making it,' Spit in the Chips replied. 'My brother in law is here from Scotland for the weekend, he's going to join us. Columbo, this is Jim; he fucking buried his wife last week, just here for a wee break'

'Lucky bastard' Wing whispered into Peter's ear. Further proof that nothing he heard in Whitehead could surprise him anymore.

Over the introductions it was established that Jim lived just a few miles from Carnoustie, in Scotland, arguably the hardest links golf course in the U.K. What was not established at this time, that would soon become embarrassingly obvious, was that Jim did not play golf.

Another two rounds of drinks was duly ordered and consumed before all four made their way to the locker room, swapped bar shoes for golf shoes, and made their way to the first tee.

Jim the visitor had been given a spare set of golf clubs by his brother in law, and as it was soon to transpire it would not have mattered if he had been given left hand or right hand clubs, or indeed the broken oar from a rowing boat. The four golfers that had teed off ten minutes in front of them were well out of driving distance and Peter, Wing and Spit in the Chips wasted no time in teeing off. Jim came to the tee box and placed his golf ball atop a tee, looked up the fairway, down at the golf ball, up the fairway, and down again at the golf ball. He positioned himself parallel to the ball while his three playing partners looked at each other, speechless, shrugging their shoulders. He shifted his feet and looked up the fairway again. Time seemed to stand still, the leaves blowing across the fairway in front of them like prairie bush blowing through the streets of a deserted Western town.

'You will need a stick' said Spit in the Chips, saving Jim's embarrassment for only a moment as he handed him a driver from his golf bag.

'Aye, aye, just sizing it up' Jim said as he took hold of the club, unsure exactly which way to hold it at first. A further several minutes were wasted while Jim continued to 'size up' and the next four golfers had arrived at the tee box, eager to tee off. There was silence around the tee box as Jim swung the club back slowly, with what those present would later describe as an impressive back swing. He swung the club and his body forward with a ferocity and speed that was completely alien to his rhythmic, smooth, backswing, and caused him to fall over on the tee box. Golfing etiquette prevented anyone present making any comment other than, 'unlucky there Jim.' Wing was gripping Peter's arm, finding it almost impossible to stifle his laughter.

'Where did it go' said Jim, using the driver as a crutch to get to his feet, looking up the fairway for the golf ball.

'Still on the tee Jim.'

Undeterred, Jim again went through his agonisingly long set up and practice routine. All seemed perfect, the backswing and follow through were sublime, a joy to watch for any

57

aficionado of the great game. Jim set up again, this time to employ his practice swing to propel the golf ball up the fairway. Unfortunately, as before, the smooth measured tempo of the backswing was followed by a frenzied, uncontrolled follow through. Tiger Woods transitioned into a dervish. The head of Jim's driver struck the front of the ball at such an acute angle it propelled the ball backwards, narrowly missing the waiting golfers, sending it into the car park, bouncing off the roofs and bonnets of parked cars before becoming lost to view. All present would later agree they had never, and would never, see a golf shot like that again.

As it was not competition golf, Jim merely gave up on the first hole, and accompanied the other three golfers as they completed their putts on the first green. Spit in the Chips had been coaching his brother in law as they walked the first fairway, offering words of encouragement. At the second tee box Peter, Wing and Spit in the Chips drove their balls up the middle of the fairway and jostled to try and find a safe position to stand while Jim went through his practice routine.

'Keep the head down Jim, eyes on the ball.'

No one knew what to expect, not the least Jim. The only positive thing that can be said about Jim's third attempt at driving was that it was consistent with the previous two. On this occasion though the club face made contact with the back of the ball, but unfortunately causing a slice that sent the ball high but violently right in the air, coming to rest on the third fairway that ran parallel to the second.

'Unlucky mate.'

Jim set off to the adjoining third fairway while his three companions strode up the middle of the second. Jim happened upon a golf ball in the middle of the third fairway. He could see the golfers that were playing in front of his four ball walking down the third fairway towards him. He decided to forego his normal laborious set up and practice routine so as not to hold up the approaching golfers. There was still around two hundred yards remaining to reach the second green. He blindly picked a club from his bag without checking to see which weapon of torture he held in his hands. He had, perhaps fortuitously, selected a putter and was able with a full swing to propel the ball 50 yards with arrow like precision back onto the second fairway. Pleased with this achievement, he used the putter to mimic the loading of a pump action shotgun before returning it to the golf bag and making his way back to the second fairway to join his playing partners. 'Getting better son,' he said to himself. He then heard a shout from a player on the third fairway.

'Excuse me, you have mistakenly played my ball, this is yours,' said the golfer, pointing towards a golf ball on the third fairway, around 50 yards away from where Jim had just played his shot of the day.

'Sorry for that boss, you just play mine, I don't mind, no harm done,' Jim shouted in response. He continued walking; assuming that his polite offer had brought a satisfactory end to the matter.

'Wait, that's not allowed,' said the approaching golfer, strutting towards him as if on a catwalk, modelling matching pink pringle trousers and polo shirt. 'You have to return my golf ball............,' and before he could finish Jim picked up the golf ball from the second fairway and threw it towards him.

'Can you throw mine back this way boss,' said Jim, expecting the favour to be returned.

'No, you have to play your ball from where it is now.'

Jim was becoming a bit exasperated now. He could see Wing, Peter, and his brother in law were already on the second green, and he was falling behind. He was only asking for his fucking ball back. As he began his walk across the third fairway to collect his golf ball the man in pink caught up with him and handed Jim the golf ball he had mistakenly struck, but politely returned.

'You have to place the ball on the fairway exactly at the place where you think you just played it from.'

Jim was now convinced that the fucking pink blancmange was taking the piss, and visitor or not his patience was running thin. Still, in order to assuage him, Jim took a few purposeful strides, stopped, and threw the ball back onto the fairway.

'No, no, you have to place the ball.'

'Fucking listen to me pinko, I have had just about enough of your Irish shit. I do the decent thing and you take the piss. Play the fucking game boss.'

And so it came to pass, twenty minutes after leaving the first tee box, and following the intervention of two golf course marshalls, Peter, Wing, Spit in the Chips, and his brother in law Jim found themselves walking back towards the clubhouse and members bar. Ulster/Scots relations had reached an all-time low.

As they approached the clubhouse they could see Wardrobe, he was on his knees at the railings near to the entrance, along with 8 or 9 others. The dogs tied to the railings were barking and straining at their leashes; but not all of them as Peter and the others were soon to find out. As they got closer it could be seen that Andy, an elderly retired shipyard worker who liked to remind everyone he met that he had a steel plate in his head, was screaming like a banshee. He was leaning against the railing, inconsolable despite the attempts of the fellow drinkers who had vacated the bar.

'Fuck me, the bar must be shut,' Wing said with a sense of alarm in his voice. The other 3 golfers said nothing, but fear was spreading through them.

'What's up Wardrobe,' Peter asked, frightened to ask if the bar was closed.

'Walked up here for a cure because Hitler's handmaiden has hid the car keys, across the car park and a fucking golf ball whizzed past, nearly took the head off my shoulders, heard it hit a few cars then it hit Andy's wee rat dog on its head and down it went. Fucking deceased.'

On hearing this recounted Andy keeled over and started sobbing uncontrollably. Someone shouted that they were going into the bar to get Andy a double whisky.

'Thank fuck for that,' Wing whispered out of respect for Andy's dead dog.

Andy was handed a large tumbler of whisky. The assembled bar crowd were baying, trying to identify the idiot who had hit the golf ball that brought a premature end to Andy's rat dog. The layout of the course was designed so that no ball flight would occur in the area of the car park and clubhouse.

'Should have had a plate in its wee head like the owner,' Wing whispered.

'Columbo, did you guys see anything on the way in,' someone from the crowd asked.

Peter, Spit in the Chips, Jim and Wing looked at each other without speaking.

'Nothing at all. No. We didn't see anyone messing about, probably kids eh.'

'Wee bastards,' said Andy, emboldened by the effects of the whisky. 'Don't they know I have a fucking plate in my head.'

Wardrobe picked up Andy's wee rat dog, cradled it in his arms, and brought it close to Andy. 'Say goodbye to Zorro for one last time Andy, can't let you suffer any longer, I will take care of him now.' A respectful silence was observed while Andy wiped the tears from his eyes, bent down, kissed his dog, and removed the collar and lead.

'Wonder why he did that,' Wing whispered.

'Probably keep it for the next dog,' said Jim the dog murderer.

'Don't know what you work at in Scotland Jim but have you considered being a Dog Warden'

'Nah that would interfere with my volunteer work with the SSPCA you prick'

No one could remember who made the call, but as Wardrobe was dumping the dead rat dog carcass into the wheelie food bin at the rear door to the kitchen a shout went up for a wake to begin. Wardrobe withdrew the carcass, now covered in waste food which he was frantically wiping off as best he could, when the shout for a wake was addressed by Turpin.

'Boys, we all share Andy's grief, and it's only right and fitting we have a wake now, but for Health and Safety we can't have Zorro present.'

Everyone assembled agreed, not only for health and safety reasons, but to stop some of the serious arse hole members from complaining. Satisfied that Zorro's presence wasn't required, Wardrobe returned him to the wheelie bin, burying the corpse under layers of rotting food. Everyone returned to the members lounge where they placed a number of tables together to establish the boundaries of the wake group, visitors were of course welcome to pay their respect and buy drink. Spit in the Chips agreed with Peter and Wing that he and his brother in law Jim would be okay for around 4 hours before the group that stood in awe at Jim's wayward golf shot returned to the clubhouse and recounted what they had witnessed to those assembled in grief. Jim was boarding the ferry back to Scotland the following morning so would escape the lynch mob that might be expected to descend on Spit in the Chips house. The Ulster – Scots relationship already soured by the incident involving Jim and the pink blancmange would be further muddied when Jim was identified as Zorro's killer.

Wardrobe brought an unused pint glass from the bar. 'Right twenty quid in each and I will put it behind the bar. Turpin will tell us when it is running out.'

'Leave it with Turpin and it will run out quicker than the black stuff from an Arab fucking oil well,' Wing said intelligently. No one said anything, but everyone tacitly agreed, and the pint glass was left on a table in full view of those gathered in sorrow. Andy was urged by all present not to contribute. It was amazing to everyone how that gesture so rapidly improved Andy's mood.

Drinks were ordered and everyone staked out their territory, giving no thought to what impact the consumption of alcohol at this early time in the morning would have on the rest of their day. It was after all an occasion that demanded that normal protocol, and long held engagements and arrangements were unselfishly put to one side in order to share the grief, and in some way shoulder some of the burden that Andy himself carried at this time.

Peter had arranged for Anne to come to the golf club for lunch. Wardrobe's wife was in London with the kids contemplating whether they had a future together or not. The potentially life changing sabbatical that his family had embarked on, that so wrecked him with guilt since their departure, had now been obliterated from his memory, he was living in the moment.

Wing, a 60 year old bachelor and white van driver by trade, lived with his Thai wife in the town. He went to Thailand every year in order to purchase and bring back suitcases full of counterfeit designer clothing for resale in the less than fashionable nearby resort areas of Larne and Carrickfergus. On his last visit to Thailand he purchased Wung from his favourite brothel. It being impossible to fit her into a suitcase he married her, promised to love her long time, and brought her back to meet his shocked, devout, catholic parents. Wung was much younger than Wing, by 40 years exactly. Wing never bothered if he failed to adhere to any plans he had made with Wung and Wung didn't bother too much either. Wing had a beautiful young wife and Wung had an insurance policy for her extended family in Thailand. Wing inherited his new nickname only after he brought Wung to the town.

Spit in the Chips and Jim were going to depart after a couple of hours in order to avoid the inevitable fall out when the truth of how Zorro met his death was discovered.

Time was not of the essence. For anyone present to depart in order to consider honouring previously arranged engagements would have been regarded as disrespectful to Andy, and the memory of Zorro, unless of course you were absolutely, falling down, pissed. The disrespect to Andy and Zorro would of course be repaid by weeks of scorn and piss taking.

Peter made as if heading to the toilets but sneaked into the locker room to phone Anne and forewarn her of what was likely to happen over the next few hours before she arrived. As she was no stranger to this sort of behaviour she was both ambivalent and accepting, with one caveat.

'Just make sure you don't fall asleep as soon as we get back to your place Romeo.'

Peter woke the next morning at the usual time, awake, but not wishing to open his eyes. He had no recollection of the previous night's events. He reached his left arm out across the bed in search for the naked form of Anne but she was not there. He rolled across the bed and inhaled, expecting to detect the aroma of her perfume, the smell of her body in the mornings that he so loved. There was nothing. He was alone. His lips were firmly stuck together, the inside of his mouth parched from lack of saliva. He managed to prise open his lips and the smell of his breath made him reel backwards to his side of the bed. He tried to piece together the events of the previous day but could not progress beyond re-joining the mourners after making a phone call to Anne.

'Oh fuck, fuck, fuck.'

He opened his eyes and stood up, the bedroom curtains had not been closed, and his clothes lay in a pile at the bedroom door, with the exception of his socks which were still on his feet. He looked out of the bedroom window to see that his car was parked in the driveway.

'Fuck, fuck.'

He could hear his phone emit a beep indicating that he had messages waiting, or had missed a call.

'Fuck.'

It was time for a mug of green tea, his favourite morning beverage, consumed because he believed in its detoxification powers. He wandered back to the bedroom, restorative mug of green tea in hand. On the way he found the phone at the bottom of the pile of clothes, and it took a few seconds for his watery eyes to focus on the screen. He had a message waiting from Anne, but no missed calls. Various scenarios were running through his mind, all concluding with the assumption that he was in real shit this time. He sat down on the bed, looked down at his feet, and could not remember putting his socks on before going to the kitchen to make his tea, whilst unable to consider why he would do so in the first place. He didn't want to open the message from Anne, and he certainly was not going to phone her until he knew exactly how the night had unfolded. Why was she not there? Had they had an argument? Was there a scene in the golf club? Had he gone too far this time and the relationship was now over?

He shaved, showered and ate his fruit based muesli in a hurry. The muesli was another healthy product that Peter thought counteracted the effects of too much alcohol. He was unusually flustered, in a rush to discover the what, when, why and how of last night.

He phoned Wing in the hope that he might fill in the many blanks but there was no reply to his mobile number. It was still early on a Sunday morning but he knew Wing never slept late so he tried the home phone number.

'Wung now on phone talking'

'Hi Wung, its Columbo here, is Wing there'

'No Mr Cumbo, he is with the sleep now'

'Wung, ask him to ring me when he gets up please'

'Wait Mr Cumbo, you lucky, he now erect himself, here he coming'

'Shit, I can leave this until later, get him to phone when you are finished.'

'Mr Cumbo, why you no marry my sista.'

Peter had never met Wungs sister; she had merely thrust a photograph of her in front of his face shortly after being introduced. The photograph had the words, 'with all my luv' scrawled along the bottom. It was no doubt intended for mass distribution. Before Peter could reply Wing seized the telephone.

'Wow that was a fucking mental one.'

'Oh yes, tell me about it. I mean just that, what the fuck happened, no sign of Anne this morning, car is in the driveway.'

Wing was renowned for his memory recall. No matter how drunk, no matter at what time the party began or ended, Wing was able to recount every moment in detail. This was a highly desirable skill for which he was much admired, and constantly called upon early on post party mornings.

'Relax Columbo, Anne couldn't make it. Do you not remember her phoning to tell you her washing machine had leaked all over the kitchen floor and she had to stay at home, clear up and wait until her Dad's friend came round to fix it.'

'Oh Aye, that's right,' but Peter and Wing both knew that Peter had no recollection of the call.

'And then you danced up to the bar and called a juniper berry failure after the mourning beer kitty had run out.'

'Aye, of course,' said Peter, digging as far as he could into the memory bank.

'And I ended up paying for the bloody Gin Columbo so you owe me nearly 40 quid.'

'Now I know you are lying, fuck off Wing.'

Being now more knowledgeable of the previous night's events Peter felt emboldened to ring Anne, only after checking that she had phoned him at 7.43pm.

'Hi wee bird, how are you and the washing machine.'

'Both needing serviced badly, sorry I couldn't come down last night Pete, Dad is in Turkey watching Northern Ireland playing and it took ages to find the number for his mate. Then I had to wait on him coming round it wasn't worth it, and it sounded like you guys were well ahead of me anyway.'

'Nah, not really, it turned out a bit of a quiet night after a lively start. I left pretty sober, I was home about 10pm.'

'Please tell me you didn't drive Pete.'

'Ah for Christ's sake no Anne, Wing's taxi dropped me off. I am just walking up for the car in a minute or so.'

Peter knew he was lying, Anne suspected he may be.

'You want to come to mine tonight, easier for you getting to North Queen Street in the morning.'

'That sounds like a plan, Indian delivery, wee bottle of wine and lots of bed.'

'You know how to win a woman over. See you around 5ish.'

Peter knew he had a few unchecked hours of drinking with friends before driving to Anne's and pass himself off as sober. Staying at Anne's gave his liver and kidneys some small respite.

Peter still enjoyed going to work after a few days off. He enjoyed not knowing what incidents he was going to attend; if he had to go to Castlereagh to interview terrorist prisoners, or a quiet day in the office catching up with reports. Sometimes listening to local radio reporting on terrorist incidents on the drive to the police station would alert him to how his day, indeed week, might be affected.

CHAPTER SIX – LATE SHIFT AT CARRICFERGUS POLICE STATION

Despite trying different continental and American based shift patterns designed to improve the welfare of personnel the P.S.N.I. reverted to the mind numbingly boring, soul destroying, and life shortening rota of seven days of early, late and night shifts.

Late shifts worked from 3pm to 11pm, and Des paraded for duty at Carrickfergus Police Station at 2.45pm on Saturday for what was to be his last late shift before beginning his C.I.D. secondment. Des had always been a car freak, and devoted great care and attention to the Volkswagen Golf GTI he had bought during his police training. He had however driven to work this afternoon in his new car, a used BMW Z4 two seater sports car that had been suggested by his mum, and mainly financed by his mum and Uncle Reg. Des had inherited his mother's Walter Mitty like characteristic. When Des told her of his impending C.I.D. secondment, she by proxy saw Des in the form of Don Johnston in Miami Vice. Des gleefully accepted the notion of the car, but unusually stood up to his mother and forbade her to buy the white linen suit she had earmarked in T.K. Max.

Alison Reid the Section Sergeant enjoyed Late Shift duties, especially at weekends when no senior officers were present in the station. The briefing to her section and life in general became more relaxed. Ronnie as ever was assigned Station Duty Officer, and Des was paired with Gus to perform mobile patrol duties, whilst the others tended to the front gate and walking beats.

Gus had joined the Royal Ulster Constabulary by virtue of his prodigious footballing talent. As a teenager he had played for short periods with Queens Park Rangers and Arsenal football clubs. Many footballing scouts had predicted he was the new George Best, quite probably possessed of greater skills, twice the drinking capacity, but half the brain. Sadly for football, but as a benefit to his longevity, Gus was crippled by parochialism. Despite the history of the great Irish diaspora, many Irish people felt uneasy about leaving its shores for anything more than brief holidays, and this was nothing to do with an abundant potato crop.

Gus returned and played for local Northern Ireland clubs, as well as Northern Ireland itself. The wages however were not commensurate with his talents, so after being approached by the manager of the P.S.N.I. football team he agreed a deal that enabled him to become a police officer who performed negligible duties, but received a regular salary with benefits. He was captain of the P.S.N.I. football team, duty bound to commit himself to front line policing duties during the closed season, with the exception of lengthy training periods. Gus spent more time in shorts and football boots than he did uniform.

Gus was from Larne, as previously mentioned a town that anyone who had wanted to commit suicide but lacked the courage would only need to visit for a day to find the commitment. He lacked social airs and graces; he lacked basic English language skills, he especially enjoyed punching people for fun, he was in short as thick as shit. But his footballing skills transcended all of these shortcomings. Even Ronnie had a grudging respect for him, despite being hospitalised overnight when Gus gave him a playful punch in the kidneys that led to internal bleeding at the last C Section social night out.

'Well Des, looks like me and you are the A team for tonight, are you an authorised driver.'

'Yes Gus, for everything except vans and HGVs.'

'Grab the keys and see you in the canteen with your kit.'

Des had all but got over the embarrassment Gus had caused him when he paraded for his first night shift at Carrickfergus Police Station, and Gus was partnered with him in the first response vehicle. At 0200hr, as was Sergeant Reid's practice, both vehicle crews came in for a break together until 0400hr. A different movie was played each night in the TV room, or you could choose simply to sleep for the two hours.

'Right Des, Sarge is off on monthly rest day tonight so the guys have got a porn movie to watch, you okay with that?'

'Yes, sure.' Des quickly replied out of sheer desperation to fit in, and also to watch a porn movie.

'Des, we are all grown men here, no policewomen, do not be surprised if some of the guys get a bit excited watching the movie if you know what I mean.'

'Yeah, no problem, cool with that.'

After shedding his body armour and collecting the packed lunch box that his mother had meticulously prepared, he made his way into the TV room. It was dark, lit only by the glow from the large screen, furnished with four rows of hideous armless chairs. The rest of C Section had spread themselves around the first three rows, leaving the entire rear row for Des. Des started eating the contents of his lunchbox as the porn movie started. He was hungry, and enjoying every morsel, savouring every bite, until the movie almost immediately switched to the scene of a mass orgy in progress. Des thought he was going to choke on his lobster salad and set his lunchbox, barley consumed, on the adjacent chair. The TV screen projected just enough glow for Des to see the vague outline of his colleagues in front of him as the porn movie continued. He glanced at several of their prostrate figures on the chairs, darkened but clear figures, and then startled he stared as best he could in utter disbelief. They had their cocks out of their trouser zips and were masturbating while watching the porn movie. Des by this stage had something of an erection himself, stretched himself back on his chair, unzipped his trousers and proceeded to masturbate while watching the movie. This was taking 'fitting in' to such a wrong level but he didn't care. After several minutes of extreme pleasure the TV room lights were switched on, darkness became light, and Des instinctively close his eyes at the shock of the flood of light. When he reopened his eyes, his penis standing erect outside of his trousers, the rest of C Section were standing up, removing large pork sausages from their trouser zips, and rounding on Des. It was a long first night shift for Des.

What Gus lacked in brains he more than made up for in good looks. His grandparents were Italian and he had inherited a swarthy complexion and jet black hair. He was 6 feet two inches tall and could easily have graced any catwalk or movie screen. Alas for Gus it would have needed to be a silent movie, as the moment he opened his mouth and mumbled, that old movie star image crumbled. Gus's pronunciations unfortunately resembled that of a stroke victim in recovery. Amazingly for a serial adulterer Gus was still married to his first love. He did however put that relationship to the test throughout the continuation of his marriage.

Des was elated. He had never been on duty with Gus before, and he had never driven the patrol vehicle except when unaccompanied on routine administrative tasks. Now he was going behind the wheel of the main response vehicle. He and Gus were Batman and Robin for the Carrickfergus late shift. Of course Batman was the true hero of the Gotham City crime busting duo, but he depended on Robin to get him to the scene quickly and safely, and of course weighed in with his disproportionate build to fight ratio when Batman was being outnumbered. As a team they had tremendous success, in fact a zero failure rating.

'Well, bring it on,' Des said to himself as he collected his personal body armour and riot helmet from his locker. 'The Joker would be making a big mistake if he came to Carrickfergus tonight.' Des dreamed of a long pursuit of a stolen vehicle, masterfully steering the response vehicle through red lights and stop signs, wiping the sweat from his brow as he purposefully avoided women carelessly crossing the road with children in prams, driving as if a master charioteer in a roman arena, displaying his skills and receiving the adulation of the audience by way of a standing ovation.

'Right Des, quick tour of the town and then take me down to the Marina. I have a witness statement to take, part of a lengthy investigation, you drop me off there and I will give you a call when I am finished.'

Even Des knew that Gus never took on any investigations, he was never in the station long enough to handle any police related work. Des grinned in smug appreciation that even he had submitted more prosecution files than Gus.

Des checked the speedometer reading on the car, and then started to check the oil and water levels as demanded by police protocol.

'Fuck sake Des, just drive the fucking thing, night shift will be taking over in a minute.'

Des hurriedly closed the bonnet and positioned himself in the driving seat. He took several minutes sliding the driver's seat back and forwards to attain the position best suited for him, while adjusting the rear view mirror at the same time. It was never like this in the bat cave. Batman and Robin ran towards their car and slipped effortlessly into their seats and sped off without any need for adjustment and thus arrived at crime scenes without delay. Des realised that Carrickfergus was never going to experience the same level of violent crime that occurred in Gotham City. He did think that Ben and Joe should at least contribute by having the response vehicle prepared and ready as if just leaving a pit stop after a four second tyre change.

Des found his perfect driving seat position and looked towards Gus; he was nearly knocked back by the smell of his expensive aftershave.

'That's a nice one Gus, is that some sort of Brut or Old Spice.'

'No son, got it from a trolley dolly, some sort of Himalaya shit, has the women hauling off their knickers as soon as they smell it.'

Des had only worked with Gus once before but knew from others that he was a womaniser, despite having a beautiful wife at home. Des secretly hoped he might learn a thing or two from Gus in the female department. Gus had already made the phone call and Moira was waiting for him at her townhouse in Carrickfergus Marina. Gus had experienced too many close shaves, scaled down too many drain pipes in fleeing from the unexpected return of a husband or boyfriend that he now only selected single females, or married as long as the husband worked away from home. Moira was of the latter category. Moira's husband worked on the North Sea oil rigs, month on month off, and allowed her to enjoy an enviable lifestyle. Childless, with a jack russell dog as a substitute, approaching forty, she was nearer to average than stunning on Gus's scale of good looks. She possessed an outstanding quality which Gus greatly admired - she loved sex, Gus assessed her as a border line nymphomaniac. She never asked to be wined and dined, never sought any romantic attachment, she merely craved sex. Too often over the many years that he had practiced infidelity he had met women who wanted some form of commitment, contact beyond sex, post coital cuddles, friendship even. Women never failed to amaze him. Gus suspected that he was not the only provider of satisfaction for Moira but he did not care.

'Just here Des, number 42. I will take a radio but this is a bit of a sensitive job so will ring you on your mobile when I am ready. Don't want to reveal too much by radio, compromise the whole thing.'

Des wished Gus would just tell the truth with a little bit of detail thrown in so that he could imagine the salacious goings on inside number 42. As he drove away he felt his penis swell inside his uniform trousers. He so wanted to get into the police station toilets but did not want to risk going back to the station without Gus. Gus was getting what Des could only fantasise about, and to make things worse he couldn't even have a wank thinking about it.

The door opened slowly in response to Gus's knock as Moira concealed herself behind it. Her jack russell dog started barking but stopped on recognising Gus. Thank goodness they could not talk. Only when the door closed could Gus fully appreciate the spectacle in front of him. Moira wore black stockings and suspenders, stilettos, and a black peep hole bra. She wore no knickers and the black triangle of her pubic hair was a truly beautiful contribution to the whole ensemble.

'Fuck me Moira, the full 57 pattern webbing, you are one horny bitch.'

'Never mind fucking you, get into the bedroom and fuck me Italian stallion.'

'Do you want a bit of fumble and foreplay first,' Gus asked as she led him to the spare bedroom.

'You better believe it Valentino, if you don't leave me here drenched in sweat with a throbbing fanny and exhausted then you have failed me.'

'That would never do, a chap has his reputation to think about.'

Moira closed the bedroom door to exclude Tiny her dog from acts of voyeurism. She also didn't want the dog to know she was a cheating adulteress. Tiny had beaten her to it and was hiding underneath the bed, curious to know what his owner got up to during the noisy sessions she conducted in the spare bedroom with numerous visitors.

Foreplay over Gus was now on top of and deep inside Moira. They kissed passionately and frantically as Gus thrust his penis faster and harder inside her. They were now both drenched in sweat, the aroma of sex swept over them. Gus slowed down, deliberately almost withdrawing his penis before letting it slide fully back inside of her. Moira was ecstatic, her hands gliding over Gus's body, face and hair. She had a sensual touch and nowhere was off limits. As Gus continued the slow rhythmic withdrawal and penetration he felt a sensation to his testicles that he had never experienced before. It was truly orgasmic, and occurred each time he withdrew and paused slightly before fully re-entering.

'Fuck Moira, you just get better and better,' he managed to splutter in between exertions. He looked down expecting to see her hands intimately caressing his testicles. He was momentarily shocked to see Tiny the jack russell on the bed between his legs, licking Gus's testicles each time he withdrew and paused. The dog had an erection that resembled a small pink lipstick. He thought quickly of kicking the dog from the bed but the heightened sexual arousal he was experiencing meant he dismissed the idea immediately. The thought that the dog, his taste buds scintillated by the taste of sweat from Gus's testicles, might then progress to the main course and actually attempt to eat Gus's testicles never occurred to him.

Gus quickly showered, splashed himself with some of Moira's husbands expensive after shave and walked out to meet the waiting Des.

'Good timing Des my son, just time to pick up something to eat and then cards.'

'I preferred the earlier after shave Gus, you know that Himalaya one'

'In a crisis situation you have to adapt and make use of whatever is available Des.'

Normally only one unit at a time would come into the station for coffee and meal breaks but at weekends on late shift, and each night on night shift, Sergeant Reid preferred that the whole shift took their break at the same time. During those shift timings it was unlikely that any senior officers would be visiting the station, with the exception of course of the stuttering Napoleon Brett Mayne. The sole reason for this was to devote an hour at least, to card playing, estimation whist in particular, each game demanding a one pound stake. The mechanics of the game were simple enough. The deal alternated and the player to the dealers left would tell the scorer how many tricks he thought he could win, and so on until the last player to call who had to call a number that ensured someone had to be wrong. That is to say if seven cards had been dealt, and six tricks called prior to the last player, the last player could not call one trick, otherwise the game could continue endlessly. A bit of strategy and bluffing was involved, but that mostly took second place to personal card table vendettas.

Des, despite several attempts at coaching, could not master the basic rule. Sergeant Reid, Ronnie, Gus, Tony Stockman and the rest of the section simply ran out of patience, and it was unanimously agreed by all, in particular Des that he would perform station security duties by manning the front gate and security sangar during these times. This allowed Des to engage in private activities of his own. It truly was a solution that suited everyone.

'Ronnie, you score the first game, six of us here so I will start the dealing on seven cards,' Sergeant Reid said as the others present removed body armour, ties, and unbuttoned shirt collars. Numerous exchanges took place about who didn't want to sit beside whom as chairs were shuffled around the adjoined canteen tables. Seating preference was not due to long standing disputes or ill will, but merely based on card playing decisions made in the previous game.

Ronnie unfolded a bespoke Microsoft word table score sheet on A4 paper that he had himself prepared, and warned everyone that no foodstuffs were allowed to be placed on, or eaten over the playing surface.

'Yeah, yeah Ronnie we know the rules by now,' said Tony Stockman, the Reserve Constable normally charged with station security. Tony slouched back in his chair, he had jet black eyebrows, well in fact under closer scrutiny it was actually one continual long eye brow over both eyes, and a jet black moustache. He looked uncannily like a Mississippi paddle boat card shark from the Western age.

Tony was last player to call and asked Ronnie how many tricks had been called already.

'It's not difficult to pay attention Anthony, eight tricks have been called so you can go anything you want, we are over called by one trick at this moment.'

'Well thank you John Ogden Nash, I will go for three.'

This was met with a chorus of dismay and derision. 'Why are you calling three when we are one over? He's fucking things up already.'

'He can call what he wants' said Sergeant Reid, 'it's you to start Gus.'

'How many did I call Ronnie'?

'Think about it Gus, it was a decision you came to thirty seconds ago after too much time spent in confused consideration, and shouted twice in my direction in a Eureka moment. Coming back to you is it.'

'Yeah that's right I went for two.'

'For the sake of good God,' said Tony the atheist, 'it wasn't that long ago a monkey took a space craft to the moon.'

'But have you ever seen a monkey play estimation.'

The banter and interruptions were an accepted part of the game and everyone wallowed in the camaraderie. The game continued in a light hearted fashion, with the possibility of becoming animated and descending into exchanges of verbal abuse when a player deliberately sabotaged another's chance of calling correctly.

Des meanwhile occupied the security sangar at the entrance to the station. This small room occupied and elevated position over the roadway and afforded a good level of view of the carriageway in front in both directions. C.C.T.V. cameras and access control were operated here, and connected to the main station by radio and intercom. He imagined he was at the Alamo, standing side by side with Bowie and Crockett, the last line of defence to stave off the marauding hordes. He was under heavy fire, rifle and arrows. He had deflected a couple of arrows but now took one to the left shoulder. 'Bloody never saw that one coming,' he sighed, seemingly unaffected. The arrow hindered the use of his Heckler and Koch MP5 machine gun so he broke the arrow just above the head that was still buried in his flesh, and threw it away contemptuously. He raised the machine gun to his shoulder and fanned it across the carriageway, firing on automatic, being careful to prevent the barrel from rising in this fire mode, killing scores of Mexican soldiers as they advanced relentlessly. His modern superior firepower was no match for the arrows and single shot Remington rifles. In between the imaginary changing of magazines he caught site of a figure just below the sangar window and pointed the weapon downwards.

'Bloody hell they are trying to scale the wall.'

When he pointed the machine gun downwards the harsh scream of a female voice roused him from his reverie.

'For fuck sake peeler, don't shoot. I am here because of my husband.'

'It's okay, I am just testing the sights, didn't see you coming up,' Des mumbled as he opened the sangar window. 'How can I help you?'

Mrs Joanne Moore proceeded to tell Des about her separation from her husband Andy. She had left the family home after only three years of marriage, unhappy at having to be the main breadwinner for lengthy periods of time while Andy found sporadic work in local bands as a drummer. He refused full time work in the futile hope he could make it with a band. Childless because of a sperm deficiency Andy suffered, she wanted another chance at life, and motherhood. Andy continued to live in the small semi-detached family home but circumstances meant the house had recently been put up for sale. She had observed during recent contact with Andy that he seemed to be experiencing bouts of depression. Only this week he had received written notification of a divorce hearing. They still conversed a few times each week, mainly to discuss the practicalities of house sale and the division of property. Joanne had tried several times over the last week to contact Andy without success. Last night she found a message from Andy left on her answer phone earlier in the week. She said his speech was slurred, and she assumed he had been drinking too much. He threatened to kill himself if the divorce proceedings went ahead before he hung up.

'So I have been trying all day to get him Constable. No one has heard from him. I still drop round some money for him every week. The curtains in the living room and bedroom of our house are still closed; the front and back doors are locked from the inside so I can't use my keys to get in.'

'Probably just a cry for help Mrs Moore,' Des suggested, only because he had heard his more senior colleagues offer the same unqualified advice in similar circumstances.

'I would still like your help to get into the house Constable. I want to make sure he is okay.'

'I have the address Mrs Moore, what say I meet you at the house in about an hour and a half.

'Constable please, this is desperate, I want help now, what if he has done something to himself.'

'Give me a minute please Mrs Moore until I check on what calls we have outstanding.'

Des knew there were no outstanding calls, he was merely trying to avoid disrupting the card game for what would likely be a false alarm, and for which he would be ridiculed and teased without mercy.

Des rang the phone in the canteen. It rang for ages as each of the card players present did not want to disrupt their trains of thought at this crucial time approaching the end of the first game. It was eventually answered by Gus while everyone present hid their cards from the inquisitive glances of the others at the table.

'Cry for help,' Gus said after listening to Des recount Mrs Moore's story. No surprise there then Des thought to himself.

'Tell her the man who deals with suicides isn't on duty today,' shouted a voice from the canteen.

Des smiled at Mrs Moore in a reassuring way, 'just checking priorities here.'

'Have a quick spin round to the house with Des please Gus, we can delay the start of the next game until you come back,' advised Sergeant Reid.

'Leave your bloody pound for this game,' one of the protagonists shouted as Gus gathered together his discarded uniform items.

Gus was introduced to Mrs Moore, didn't much fancy what he saw, but agreed to meet her at the matrimonial home in Loughview Road. Des waited in the police car while Gus took a few minutes settling back into full uniform and body armour before joining him for the drive up North Road towards Loughview.

'For Christ sake Des, would you stop picking your nose? What are you going to do with that bloody bogey'?

Des knew what he would like to do with it, but chose instead to open the driver's door and flick it onto the roadway. Only half way through his late shift duty and Gus had deprived Des of his two greatest passions.

On arrival at the small semi-detached house Gus and Des joined Mrs Moore at the front door. Gus took charge of the situation while Des offered reassuring smiles to Mrs Moore. Gus tried ringing the doorbell several times, as well as knocking on the white plastic double glazed door. He had Mrs Moore ring the home telephone and with his ear pressed to the curtained front window he could hear the phone ringing inside. Gus knelt down and opened the letter box to peer inside. There was a small vestibule, no bigger in area than the average phone box, and he could see mail had collected there over several days. An almost opaque smoked glass door from the vestibule prevented him from seeing clearly into the hallway. As his vision adjusted he could see the silhouette of a person standing in the hallway, arms by their side, not far from the vestibule door. Gus was no Detective, but he deduced this was Mr Moore.

'Andy, it's the police here, could you open the door please.'

'Oh he is there, great Constable, he's no idea how worried he has made me.'

Des nodded and smiled at Mrs Moore as if to say 'I told you so.'

There was no movement from behind the vestibule door.

'Andy your wife is very worried about you, come on now open the door.'

Gus tried using Mrs Moore's door key but her husband had left the key inside the lock making it impossible to open the door.

'Well Mrs Moore, the situation is that we can't make him open the door. He is there, but unless you authorise us we can't force entry,' Gus said, in the hope that he may now be able to get back to the station in time for the start of the second game of cards.

'I have to get in and see him Constable and get this sorted out. If it means he has to pay to get the door fixed then it's his fault for being an arse.'

Gus stood back from the door and beckoned Des forward. 'Des, the door, one full shoulder charge should do it.' Gus ascended the three steps to the front door, turned sideways, took a step back with his right foot onto the step below and propelled himself forward with all his might. The double glazed door refused to move, unlike Des who was propelled backwards onto the pathway, knocking over Mrs Moore in an action similar to a bowling ball felling a skittle.

Gus helped Mrs Moore to her feet, unconcerned about the welfare of Des who sat stunned on the pathway, gripping his suspected dislocated shoulder.

'Right enough nonsense,' said Gus. 'You have to attack the lock, not the door frame.' Gus walked up, took careful aim, and booted the door exactly where the lock made contact with the frame. The door offered no resistance and sprung open, stopped from fully opening by the accumulation of mail on the vestibule floor. 'Still the best right foot in this country,' Gus muttered. Mrs Moore was too busy helping Des to his feet to notice the impressive progress Gus had made and he was slightly disappointed that his work had gone unnoticed.

The silhouette behind the vestibule door was similarly unmoved and Gus reached for the door handle, slowly pushed the door open while taking a step into the hallway.

'Oh fuck,' said Gus to himself. He looked round to see Mrs Moore still fussing over Des, closed the vestibule door and took a couple of steps towards Andy Moore. He had hung himself from the stair bannisters using a nylon rope which had stretched over a period of time, only stopping when Andy's feet made contact with the hall carpet. That was why his silhouette looked just like someone standing in the hallway. If he had used a normal hemp rope he would have been dangling, a clear distance would have been visible between his feet and floor even through the smoked glass door. His head was tilted to one side, his face calm and serene suggesting he did not try and fight the tightening of the noose around his neck. He had passed from the rigor mortis stage into liver mortis, highlighted by the purple and red discolouration to his skin. He was well and truly dead, and so beyond any attempts at resuscitation. A bubble of snot hung from his left nostril and drool had formed a crust on the left side of his mouth.

Gus left the hallway, closed the vestibule door, and stepped out onto the front steps just as Mrs Moore was about to step through the front door. He grabbed Mrs Moore and put his arms around her. Des didn't think that Mrs Moore would be Gus's type. For goodness sake he had only just finished with the woman in the Marina and now he had Mrs Moore in an embrace. This man was insatiable. As Des struggled to interpret what he was seeing in front of him the reality of the situation was brought home with remarkable clarity.

'Mrs Moore, your husband is dead, I am sorry to tell you he has hung himself.'

Mrs Moore tried to push Gus out of the way, clawing at his uniform, crying and screaming, demanding to see her husband. Gus held her back as lightly as he could, telling her that she couldn't get into the house, that her husband's body would eventually be removed to Foster Green Mortuary. Gus slowly motioned her into the back of the police car. He then told Des to check the inside of the house for any signs of a suicide note, pills, or empty bottles of alcohol, and not too touch the body. He used his mobile phone to contact Sergeant Reid to avoid Mrs Moore hearing the radio messages inside the car.

'Ali, he has hung himself. Looks like maybe a day at the most. Nothing suspicious but will need the usual agencies here.'

'Ah so sad, I will get uniform to call out the Forensic Medical Officer, find out which SOCO is covering and get C.I.D. to you.'

'I will leave Des at the scene and bring Mrs Moore back to the station.'

'That's fine Gus, I will get the kettle on, bring her straight to my office, not the interview room.'

Even when a body has been ripped apart by a bomb, or decapitated by a train, a doctor, normally the Forensic Medical Officer would still have to attend the scene to pronounce life extinct. It was normal procedure up until very recently that uniform police would decide if C.I.D. officers were necessary at the scene of a suicide, the act by its very nature not falling into the 'suspicious' death category. At the scene of a fatal fire in the New Lodge area of Belfast, in an area where what remained of the female corpse lay, limbs cruelly distorted in death by the intense heat, discarded cigarette ends were present near to the body, and on an armchair. The assessment by the fire service at the scene was that the fire had been started by careless disposal of cigarette ends, the armchair the most likely point where the fire took hold. Agreeing with this assessment the uniform police at the scene called the Forensic Medical Officer but dispensed with the need for C.I.D. After life was pronounced extinct, the undertakers started to lift the remains onto a mortuary zip up stretcher to reveal the charred remains of fire lighters on the floor area upon which the body had been found. Henceforth C.I.D. officers were called to every scene of a suicide, whether the cause was obvious or not.

Gus stopped at the station security sangar to leave Mrs Moore's car keys for collection by a member of her family. Tony Stockman the Reserve Constable was reclined on a chair inside.

'Is that the widow Moore you have with you Gus.'

'I swear to god Tony I will punch your fucking lights out if I ever here shit like that again.'

He spoke like Dean Martin after far too many martinis. The seriousness and intent was not lost by Gus's slow, soft delivery of his threat and Tony took it to heart immediately.

Des felt certain unease any time he had to walk past the body of Andy Moore, still connected to the stair bannisters by the nylon rope. It was as if he was watching Des searching through his house, wondering what he might find, and his eyes following his every move. The bubble of snot still hung from his nostril and was much admired by Gus. Gus moved into the kitchen having worked his way systematically from the top of the house, finishing the cursory search in the kitchen. On the breakfast bar were an empty bottle of gin and a partially finished bottle of whiskey. There was an empty used glass on the breakfast bar and fragments of a broken glass on the kitchen floor. Near the glass was an A4 sheet of paper and a felt tip pen. Des picked up and read the sheet of paper. In parts the writing was scrawled, in others more ordered, probably a sign that it had been written at different stages.

'Joanne (ex best friend, soon to be ex wife)   What a greedy, uncaring, bastard you turned out to be. All YOU, YOU, YOU, didn't give fuck about me. I hope if you do ever have kids they will be deformed and fucked up. Never hate anyonc like you – wish I had courage to kill you. I will die soon, very quick – I hope you die a slow painful death. Hope people know YOU killed me. Andy'

Des felt like a Detective who had just found the murder weapon that would help convict a serial killer.

Sergeant Reid comforted Mrs Moore, whilst at the same time slowly and discreetly extracting the personal details she needed for Gus to commence the Police Incident File, and prepare the forms necessary for the post mortem. Gus left the office to update the Central Control Room with the details; his respect for Ali Reid had increased immeasurably. He then brought Mrs Moore out to the police car for the journey to the Mortuary for the task he was dreading most; the identification of the remains of her husband by Mrs Moore.

Sergeant Reid drove to Loughview Road to ensure all relevant agencies were finishing up at the house, and that the body would be on its way to the mortuary in good time so that Mrs Moore did not have to wait about. She also had to collect Des. The body was just being loaded into the back of the undertakers van as she arrived, SOCO were just leaving, and C.I.D. had paid nothing more than a perfunctory visit. All Sergeant Reid and Des had to do now was to wait on the locksmith making a temporary repair to the front door.

'Alright Des,' asked Sergeant Reid, mindful that he had been left at the scene alone for a considerable period of time.

'Found this in the kitchen beside the drink bottles Sarge,' Des said, handing her the A4 sheet.

Sergeant Reid read the contents of the piece of paper and asked Des if he had shown it to the C.I.D. or mentioned it to anyone else.

'No Sarge, but it is good evidence of his state of mind.'

'Des, we have more than enough evidence of his state of mind. Mrs Moore does not need any more grief visited upon her by being shown this letter.'

Sergeant Reid tore the sheet of paper into shreds and put them into her pocket for later disposal.

'Des, I am asking you never to mention this letter to anyone.'

'What letter Sarge.'

'Des you truly are becoming a real policeman – and you call me Ali when there are no senior ranks about.'

'Thanks Sarge.'

CHAPTER SEVEN – BRETT AND ANGEL

Brett tried to restrict his consumption of alcohol at home because when he did partake it was normally to excess. This was a trait so out of character for the man he considered himself to be. He drank only Bordeaux red wines, and when the first sip of the deep red nectar seduced his taste buds he was powerless to resist the uncontrollable urge to constantly repeat the sensation.

He preferred a Grand Vin de Bordeaux Medoc or St Emillion, even a Laungedoc occasionally was worth slipping out of the region for. But he salivated over Grand Cru Paulliac or Pomerol for special occasions. This near orgasmic experience was normally accompanied by the finest Cuban cigar. The wine also had the near miraculous Lourdes effect of negating Brett's stutter, the more he drank the more loquacious he became, but without the stutter. Since agreeing the pact of sexual abstinence with Angel it was noticeable that Brett's indulgence for wine and cigars was more frequent and prolonged than it had been during the brief period of their coital relationship. His study, where he enjoyed most of his drinking and smoking, looked and smelled like the cigar room of a private gentleman's club, a setting that he imagined himself fitting into like a hand into a glove, with the exception that Brett was the only member in this club.

Angel too since her marriage to Brett had developed a taste for the finer things in life and thought it beneath herself and offensive to her taste buds if she drank anything other than the finest champagne. She so despised the term sparkling wine without realising it was synonymous with champagne and indeed that sparkling wine was champagne and became champagne only because it came from that region; Non-vintage Moet & Chandon was suitable for everyday drinking, but Grand Cru Veuve Clicquot was preferred at weekends, or on the rare occasions when they hosted visitors.

They unwittingly did share a common bond after all, namely a love for Grand Cru vintages

When Robert Peel Mayne was put to bed at nights by the Nanny, Angel drank in the drawing room of their large home, sometimes alone, sometimes with the Nanny, seldom with Brett. Brett would drink in his study on the first floor of their rambling Victorian house, sometimes alone, sometimes with the Nanny, never with Angel.

Tonight they were hosting Assistant Chief Constable Peter Enis and his wife Lotta. Peter was head of the Complaints and Discipline Branch in P.S.N.I. Headquarters, and a much needed confidante and friend that would enable Brett's prompt return to Headquarters Policing, hopefully by way of promotion. He had never met Peter's wife before, but had heard accounts that she was a bit of a 'bon viveur,' which he thought so out of character for both Peter and himself.

Nanny was preparing the dinner while Brett and Angel showered and dressed in their respective bedrooms before retiring each to their comfort zones of drawing room and study. Brett wore a pair of the Nanny's dental floss G strings under his weekend chinos. Boy did they feel good when he bent down and the minute string tightened inside the cheeks of his arse, tantalising the rim of his anus. What made it even better for Brett was the knowledge that he had retrieved the flimsy string from the Nanny's wash basket.

He had agreed to meet Angel at the small bar in the drawing room at 7 p.m., half an hour before Peter and Lotta Enis were due to arrive. The bar had been installed by the previous owner; it had been retrieved from an old railway station in Belfast, a relic from the Victorian days when most main railways stations had bars. The tiles from the railway station had also been carefully re-laid in the bar area and provided a pastiche of a bygone era that Brett enjoyed, hoping that visitors may think him an aficionado of antique restoration. The stools in front of the bar that were bought by Angel were low backed, chrome and black faux leather, more suited to a main street hair dressing salon. A certain type of critic might suggest the stools were so far 'out there' they actually were the perfect match for the bar, in the same way that Tracey Emin's tampon strewn bedroom was a work of art. The rest of the world's sane population would judge them as disgustingly inappropriate, not worthy of being in the same room as any piece of Victorian architecture. Brett merely accepted his wife's home design foibles for an easy life.

Peter joined Angel at the appointed time; both slightly animated by the consumption of a pre meeting drink, each now more at ease in the others company. Angel's dress sense was on a par with her excellence in home design. She always wore expensive designer clothes, scouring Belfast city centre and beyond for designer labels, paying scant if any attention to the garment the label was attached to. The fact that she was about to be presented to an Assistant Chief Constable and his wife, wearing a pink checked skirt, a ghastly green striped top and blue shoes concerned her not. Each item was expensive and bore a designer label hence the appearance must work. Brett complimented her on how she looked as he slowly extracted the cork from a bottle of Pomerol Grand Cru using his favourite waiters' friend. On top of the Nanny's g string knickers Brett wore a pair of Barbour chinos. This was matched by a brown check Barbour shirt with a red cravat, and a stout pair of brown Loake brogues. Angel wasn't in the mood to be as complimentary as her husband.

'Why do you insist on dressing like a hunting, fishing, bloody country aristocrat, we live in the city, true urbanites, postcode BT2 darling.'

There was no real edge to Angel's comment; Brett did not have to fear that his wife was going to be a social embarrassment. That she finished the remark with the word darling put him at ease.

'I dress like this Angel so that you have more money to buy the designer clothes that so suit you.'

'Remember the time you wanted to mount the deer's head with the massive antlers above the fire place in the lounge darling,' Angel smirked, putting her arm around his shoulders, renewing his confidence that she was going to behave as he wanted. He knew from experience that if he discreetly advised Angel on how he expected her to behave in front of people he wanted to impress, she would behave in the opposite, mostly embarrassing way.

'That's why I now leave all home design in your very expert and capable hands dear,' Brett responded, cringing at the feel of her arm across his shoulders, and stomach knot cringing thinking about the framed photograph of the Mayne family that now hung above the fireplace. A photograph that would easily win awkward family of the year in a U.S. red neck photographic competition

'The only rural animal life you have ever seen has been dead and rendered partially back to life by a taxidermist. And as for those stupid fishing flies you wear in your deerstalker hat, you have only ever seen trout and salmon up close in boxes at St Georges market on a Saturday darling.'

Brett was happy for the negativity to flow now, before his guests arrived. Angel knew that Brett fretted about how she would conduct herself in front of people he wanted to impress. She also knew that any advancement in career for Brett was matched commensurately by a more lavish lifestyle for her. She knew when to stop.

The Nanny was preparing a beef wellington in the kitchen. For a generous increase in salary she had taken on the role of cook in addition to her child minding duties. The pact of sexual abstinence Angel had negotiated with Brett included a clause that excused her from cooking anything in the kitchen other than by microwave, in ready meal packaging form.

The feelings they thought were love for each other in the early days of their courtship had now been replaced by rules, modes of behaviour, and tacit agreements that led to a mutual satisfaction that could not be sustained by the practices of a normal husband and wife relationship.

At 7.30 pm exactly the doorbell rang to announce the arrival of Peter and Lotta Enis. Brett checked himself in the hallway mirror, making slight adjustments to his cravat before opening the door to welcome his guests. Brett shook hands with Peter, an act he always found a bit strange, if not rather uncomfortable. Peters thumb always appeared to search about Brett's hand, as if a Harrier jump jet in flight, hovering for a place to land, until it found a suitable place in between the joints of his fingers, when Peter would then apply an excessive amount of pressure until Brett was able to wriggle his hand free. Peter then introduced Lotta who was wholly unremarkable except for her dyed pink hair and stud in her left nostril. This was an oddly curious and unexpected combination. He really had no cause to worry about Angel for the rest of the evening. As Brett bent to kiss Lotta on the cheek in welcome he detected the unmistakable aroma of gin.

At the bar in the drawing room Brett managed the introductions, but had to discreetly nudge Angel who had locked onto Lotta with a non-blinking stare that made even him feel uncomfortable. With everyone seated at the bar Brett took up the task of pouring drinks. It was the same again for him and Angel, gin and very little tonic for Lotta, and a single malt whisky for Peter, no ice or water, just a dash of diet coke. Peter's application for membership of the Whisky Appreciation Society and Club in Edinburgh had been rejected each year he had applied, but he hoped this year his name would be nearer the top of what he imagined to be a long waiting list.

The ladies huddled closer at the bar very soon after the formal introductions and engaged in frivolous small talk on subjects ranging from fashion to derelict husbands. This gave Brett a chance to engage directly with Peter before they sat down to dinner, and they immediately began to converse about the only subject of which they had any knowledge or interest – work.

'Well Brett, what is it like being in charge of a busy Sub Division with so many officers, and a diverse population.'

'Diverse officers more like, they give the Force a bad name.'

'Ha ha, just what I expected to hear from you Brett,' Peter chuckled insincerely.

'The thing is Peter; I miss the cut and thrust, and the challenge of real policing that the likes of the Ethics Department, and Complaints and Discipline bring."

'I know Brett, but this is essential for your CV and career advancement. Another six months purgatory with the cannon fodder and we will soon have you back under wraps, away from the hordes of the great unwashed, and hopefully with promotion in sight.'

This was music to Brett's ears, nothing, but nothing could remove the smug grin of satisfaction from his face. That was until Lotta interrupted his serenity by asking for another drink, 'Sambuka this time Brett my dear,' she semi slurred whilst holding out her empty gin tumbler.

'This glass will do. Heard on the radio the dreadful business of that suicide in Carrickfergus, just awful, life is far too valuable. Were you there Brett dear?'

Brett mumbled and took Lottas empty glass to the drawing room bar and reached for the nearby phone.

It was Ronnie who answered the phone call from Superintendent Brett Mayne.

'Co, Constable Bu, Butler,' said Brett, wincing when he recognised the voice, his stutter returned and in full flow.

'It's Ronnie Sir, please,' aware that the battle of minds with the stuttering Napoleon had been easily won.

'Why do I ha, have to hear on local radio of a suicide, why was I, I not called.'

'Sir the escalation cascade for dissemination of information in the Division excludes you from being bothered with such mundane matters when off duty.'

'Yes, Ro, Constable of course, slipped my mind,' Brett replied, having little idea what Ronnie was talking about.

'On the other hand Sir, if a catholic dog shits on a protestant footpath, or vice versa, I have to inform you.'

Brett hung up the phone a defeated man.

Brett, unfamiliar with alcohol measures, poured a tumbler of Sambuka for Lotta, and was pleased when he returned that the ladies attention had easily drifted to another mundane topic. The starter and main courses of dinner were served and the only interruption to the talk around the table was when Brett had to replenish Lotta's tumbler with differing types of alcohol. Finally, just as Nanny brought in the dessert, the excessive accumulation of varying types of alcohol finally caught up with Lotta's brain, and she slumped slowly forward from the waist, her head appeared to float downwards, almost hovering at times looking for a place to land before coming slowly to rest onto the empty dinner plate from which she had only recently consumed her beef wellington. Brett and Angel were aghast and momentarily speechless.

'Will we call an ambulance,' Angel eventually suggested, staring unblinkingly at the pink shock of hair soaking up what was left of the gravy on Lotta's plate.

'Should we check her pulse and airways,' suggested Brett, knowing that he lacked the knowledge to do so.

'No not at all,' cried Peter, indicating to Brett that his whisky glass was empty. 'Creature of habit that girl, she'll be fine in 15 minutes or so, trust me.' Brett and Angel continued rather uncomfortably with dessert and what conversation they could muster. Peter continued unabated, obviously accustomed to eating while his wife was in a comatose state next to him.

Nanny was still holding the dessert intended for Lotta, 'Shall I put this in the fridge for Lotta for when she wakes up?'

'Goodness no, she will probably just ask for a drink,' replied Peter knowledgeably.

Dinner over, and Lotta's repose seemingly far from over, Brett, Angel and Peter retired to the bar in the drawing room where they could see into the dining room through the open Victorian double doors. It was 10 pm and Peter's driver was due to collect him and his wife at 10.30 pm.

'Would you like a glass of port and a rather nice cigar Peter,' asked Brett grovelingly, causing Angel to turn her eyes upwards in disdain, aware that there was no chance of the men going outside of her chintz drawing room to exhale the cigar smoke.

'Is the pope a Catholic,' Peter replied, convulsed by laughter and alcohol at his own witty response.

Brett located the bottle of Late Bottled Vintage port from behind the bar, removed the obstructive protection around the neck of the bottle, and slowly removed the cork from the bottle, causing only the slightest 'pop' to emanate. As he did this Lotta sat bolt upright on her seat at the dining table, her pink hair showing some small signs of gravy staining, and demanded, 'Just use the same tumbler for the port Brett dear, and I'll have a cigar too as long as it's not Cuban, hate what that bugger Castro has done to the country.'

What little remained of the evening passed in relative calm compared to what had gone on previously. Peters transport arrived and after bidding farewells at the front door Lotta walked to the car first and could be heard instructing the driver that they were heading to the Rugby Club. Peter lingered, turned Brett slightly to one side and said, 'What happens at dinner parties stays at dinner parties if you know what I mean Brett. Wouldn't want to delay your return to Headquarters.'

CHAPTER EIGHT – C.I.D. SECONDMENT

Peter was more relieved than normal to get to the CID Office in plenty of time for his early shift. His relationship with Anne was relaxed and almost informal, although everyone regarded them as a couple, and social invitations and greetings cards were addressed to them both. Peter was content with this state of affairs, but he knew Anne wanted to proceed to a more formalised relationship. Peter relished his regime, his fluidity of movement, and not having to be accountable to anyone. He had the strongest of feelings for Anne, but felt his real appreciation of her was borne out of her not imposing on his lifestyle. A step towards anything more serious would upset this status quo in his opinion. What he remembered of the previous evening's conversation, after she extricated him from the golf club members lounge, yet again, was talk of commitment, and a life together under one roof, rather than the separate living arrangements they now conducted. He had been able to sneak out early morning without wakening Anne, and reawakening the conversation of the night before. He knew of course that he was only delaying the inevitable.

Peter could hear Bob's voice bellowing from the tea room as he walked along the corridor towards the CID offices, regaling all present with intimate and sordid details of his recent trip to Istanbul to watch Northern Ireland suffer yet another defeat on foreign soil.

'I fucking tell you, covered in mud I was, washed off, then a massage with this fucking beauty. Dark skinned, but not a nigger, tall, stunning bod. She is wearing the clinical white stuff but you knew what was underneath. Sure enough, whipped over after the massage to my back, leg and arse for the frontal massage and I have a cock like a tent pole holding up the wee towel, couldn't miss the bloody thing.'

'Bob was this really you, or are you relating someone else's experiences.'

'Fuck off numb nut, I still got it. Anyway, she sees the big boy pushing the towel up and asks if I want a wank. Fucking right I do pet I said, hoping it's included in the price by the way. She goes off, I'm thinking she is getting rid of the nursing gear and getting the stockings and suspenders on. About 5 minutes later, my boy has gone a bit deflated and she came in

dressed as she was before and asked if I had finished my wank…….fuck me.'

Everyone in the room started to laugh and fire questions at Bob who changed the subject

immediately, and without pausing for breath when Peter entered the tea room.

'I am fucking telling yous now, I can get you a crate of two year old Bowjulays Noovo from

Stig my lorry driver mate for 25 quid, and this stuff is just getting better with age, ask the

fucking wine experts, it's all there.'

'But Bob, isn't Beaujolais Nouveau supposed to be consumed within a short time, it's not a

wine for laying down surely,' came the response from a voice Peter was unfamiliar with as

he approached the tea room.

'What the fuck would you know Hawaii 2 point fucking 5,' was the best Bob could muster in

the face of this challenge to his extensive ignorance of wine.

'I did a wine appreciation night course at the Tech, mum's idea, but I did learn a thing or two

about wine.'

'Shite is what you learned young cub, get your mammy to get the money back.'

When Peter walked into the tea room he remembered that a new aide to CID was starting

today and he was to mentor him for the three months. He had forgotten his name, but

identified him immediately as the young portly individual in the tea room wearing a light

brown linen suit. The tea room went unusually quiet, but only for the briefest of moments.

'Ah Peter lad, this is your apprentice tracker Des, hope to fuck he knows more about police

work than he does fine wine,' said Bob, braking the almost undetectable silence.

Des stood up, patting down the creases in his linen suit with no real effect, and offered his

hand to Peter, who accepted it rather limply while assessing the fat young man before him

installed in a ridiculous linen suit.

'Des, I am Peter, you are with me for the next three months, but not in that fucking suit.'

'My mums idea, sorry, is it that bad.'

'We are working in the New Lodge, a staunch IRA republican heartland, not fucking Miami

Beach, Florida.'

Peter could see Des's cheeks start to redden as he shifted uncomfortably in his seat. Bob and the others assembled in the tea room appeared to be about to launch further vitriol towards Des who they now compared to a wildebeest taking its last floundering steps at the precipice of a cliff, ahead of a descending pack of lions.

'Come into the main office Des and I will show you your desk for the next three months,' motioned Peter.

The pack of lions came to a juddering halt at the edge of the cliff, looking at each other in bewilderment, wondering where and why their prey had just been removed to safety.

Peter had an arm around Des's shoulder as he led him to the only vacant desk in the office. 'Take your jacket off, sit down and read everything I am about to give you, and don't go back into the tea room until Bob's morning ritual is over.'

Des did not respond but was gratified to be away from a group conversation that he was finding increasingly difficult to be part of in any meaningful way. He knew he was right about the wine, but had lost the argument in the face of Bob's aggressive and peremptory response.

Peter set down a folder full of Crime Report Forms, and Amendment Forms showing the latest recorded crimes and detection rates for the station area, photographs of active terrorists in the area, as well as the index to Serious Incident Reports, which greatly outnumbered the reporting of ordinary crime. Peter drew up a seat and explained to Des how different policing in North Queen Street was compared to Carrickfergus.

North Queen Street really was Fort Apache the Bronx. The external walls and windows had been reinforced with mortar proof brickwork and steel encased windows. Tall metal structures appeared sporadically in the car parking area in order to block out the view into the station yard from the three overlooking hi rise blocks which dominated the New Lodge Road, the heart of Irish Republican North Queen Street. They served not only to block the view, but to hinder aimed shooting from the flats into the station yard. The metal was pockmarked with bullet holes. Artillery House was the hi rise block nearest to New Lodge Road, and its roof space housed an Observation Post that was manned permanently by four army personnel, who spent three months in its confined environment, being serviced and supplied by helicopter whenever necessary.

Peter explained that Des would not be able to stroll out of the station and take a relaxing coffee, or shop in the local Tesco express. There was no such thing as a routine call for police officers at North Queen Street. Uniformed policing here took place in 2 or 3 fully armoured land rovers, quite often preceded by, or accompanied by military support. Every call from the local public was treated with suspicion, and in most cases considered as a lure to bring police vehicles and personnel into an area where they could be attacked by mortar, rocket, homemade coffee jar bombs, petrol bombs, gun shots or any combination thereof. Most calls during the hours of darkness were not responded to for that reason.

If a decision were made to attend a report of an incident in the area, it was never met with an immediate response. Generally the military were tasked to go into the area first and set up a secure cordon. Heavily armoured police land rovers would then deploy into the immediate area. Further armoured police land rovers would then convey CID officers to the scene of the reported incident.

'This is a shit hole Des, but I like it this way. If it doesn't suit you we can get you back to Carrickfergus.'

'I need a change Peter, and I want to learn, just give me a chance, I can fit in.'

Despite first appearances, Peter truly thought Des could do just that.

Peter started to explain to Des about the morning coffee ritual with Bob, and Bob's thinly disguised dislike of Catholic police officers when the station tannoy requested any member of the C.I.D. to contact the Station Enquiry Office on the ground floor.

Peter picked up the nearest telephone and rang downstairs.

'Hi Peter here, CID office, who's that?'

'It's Blacky, how are you mucker.'

'Blacky why did you not just ring up here rather than tannoy and give the impression we are unavailable?

'Too busy mate.'

'You wouldn't know how to spell fucking busy, what do you want.'

'There's a Sean Conlon here from 17C Artillery House, you left a calling card at his flat about six weeks ago asking him to contact you.'

'No fucking idea let me check and get back to you – if you're not too busy.'

'Fuck off, I'm busy.'

Peter had scribbled the details on a notepad and asked Des to check in the SIR's (Serious Incident Reports) for the file containing the details of the incident that he could not bring to mind immediately. As he sat racking his memory the penny dropped just as Des dropped the file onto Peter's desk.

'Ah yes, the rocket attack on the military patrol from the flat,' sighed Peter, glad that his power of recall wasn't losing him completely.

Peter, almost without the aid of the Serious Incident Report containing full details of the attack, was able to give Des a full account of what had happened, and why Sean Conlon needed to be interviewed.

A failed rocket attack on a three vehicle military patrol in the New Lodge Road had taken place from 17C Artillery House. Quite surprising in itself everyone thought at the time considering the 24/7 observation post was atop of that same block of hi rise flats. Military technology had assisted in pinpointing a general area of where the attack emanated from and Artillery House was very quickly sealed off by army personnel. The intelligence indicated an attack from a flat directly overlooking New Lodge Road from floors fifteen to nineteen. It took nearly an hour for the various security cordons to be put in place before Peter was taken to the scene assisted by RUC uniform personnel to gain entry either by consent or forcibly to search every flat on those five floors that overlooked New Lodge Road. Consent was never given. Any flats that appeared unoccupied, or whose occupants did not respond to the police knock on the door were also forcibly entered and typically of that long evening 17C was the last to be forced open. The flat was virtually empty apart from mail that had gathered in the hallway, a coffee table, a wardrobe with one door hanging off, a chest of drawers, and a discarded homemade rocket launcher lying just inside the open living room window. An electoral roll check, corroborated by the unopened mail, identified the tenant as a Sean Conlon. It looked however like nothing more than a Social Security financed mail drop. The sheer logistics in organising the army and police in order to make a return visit to 17C Artillery House restricted Peter to making only one more visit In order to try and locate the occupant, and that was when he left the calling card that Sean Conlon had shown to Blacky in the Enquiry Office. Peter could not remember the last time anyone had actually contacted him in response to a calling card request.

'Right Des, hit the ground running, get down there, get the Voluntary Attendance Form completed, and he doesn't need a solicitor.'

'How do you he doesn't need a solicitor, we haven't asked him yet.'

'Because you will convince him, otherwise you are not going to make it as a Detective.'

Des leaned as close as he comfortably could to Peter and in a whisper asked him if he could help him out just this first time with this informal approach to the legal formalities.

'Sure Des of course, much better you tell me you are not sure of something than bash ahead and make a bollocks. Let's go.'

Taking the stairs from the first floor CID office down to the Enquiry Office in seconds, Peter stopped short of the connecting door, looking through the one way glass to see only one person waiting in the Enquiry Office, obviously Sean Conlon. He was dishevelled, unwashed, physically shaking, and continually licking his lips. Peter turned left of the door and motioned to Blacky, the Station Duty Officer, behind the Enquiry Office counter and whispered, 'Conlon?' Blacky nodded in affirmation.

'Are we going to arrest him Peter, or Voluntary Attendance,' Des asked.

'Voluntary, but we will chat with him first.'

Peter and Des entered the waiting area, and rather than take Sean Conlon directly to an interview room, after introducing themselves they ushered him into a small waiting room just off the Enquiry Office. Sean handed Peter the calling card he had left some six weeks earlier, looking somehow as if a dog had chewed it and he was left with the remains.

'I know what it's about Detective; bastards used my flat to rocket the Brits. I had fuck all to do with that, I don't get involved in that stuff. I'm just an alco. Would have been here sooner but I went off the booze a few days ago and my head and body are truly fucked.'

Peter could see tears start to well up in Sean's eyes, and he was shaking uncontrollably, the front of his shirt bore stains of dried vomit.

'Honestly Detective I have been in that flat not knowing if its night or day, I see monsters coming out of the walls and ceiling, attacking me, but I need to get off the booze. I piss and shit myself and can't help it.'

Peter put his hand on Sean's shoulder, leaned closer to him and said, 'Sean son, you have enough troubles in your life right now, and I promise you I am not going to make things any harder for you. You are not being arrested; just need you to sign a wee form for me saying you came voluntarily.' Peter motioned for Des to collect the Voluntary Attendance Form booklet from Blacky while Peter brought Sean to a nearby interview room.

Des sat next to Peter at the desk and slid the Voluntary Attendance booklet in front of him. It was blank with the exception of the Voluntary Attendance number that Blacky had got from the Divisional Custody Office. Peter had written Sean's date of birth and other relevant details on an A4 sheet of paper and slid them to Des to write onto the form. As Des was doing this Peter began speaking to Sean. It occurred to Des that Peter had not administered the official police caution, or offered Sean the opportunity to consult with a solicitor, but he had at least realised not to say anything.

When Des had finished filling in the form Peter placed it in front of Sean.

'Okay Sean, if you could just sign here confirming that no way have we arrested you, you are here purely voluntarily,' indicating a line halfway down the page, 'and then just here,' pointing to a line just below the first, 'so as we don't have to waste time on solicitors, and get you away from here much quicker.'

Sean took the ballpoint pen from Peter in his right hand, but he was shaking so much he resembled a demented magician waving a wand. Sean tried to control the shaking by steadying his right hand with his left hand, but to no great avail. He hovered his right hand over the line where he was to apply his first signature, made contact with the page, but could only manage a swerve to the right and upwards at 45 degrees and off the page.

'That will do for both,' said Peter, retrieving the pen from Sean's wavering grasp.

'Right Sean, you obviously had serious booze problems, give me an idea of your intake for a normal day,' Peter asked, not altogether altruistically, but more as a comparison benchmark for himself.

'Well I would wake up, day or night time, it could be either and start on bottles of cider, maybe four or five of them.'

Peter thought a few bottles of cider was nothing much, but he quickly learned that Sean was referring to 2 litre plastic bottles of cider.

'Then I would go onto the vodka, until that ran out and back onto cider until I collapsed.'

'What did you put in your vodka?'

'Nothing, just a straight litre bottle of vodka, even more if I still had money.'

'What did you eat during all this?'

'Nothing, I just kept on drinking, collapsing and throwing up, I used to wake up day or night times.'

'Christ Sean, how are you still alive, and how are you managing to stay off the booze now,' Peter asked, very much aware that for him to stop drinking would be a Herculean task, but taking solace in the fact that his intake was nothing to worry about compared to Sean's.

'It's not been easy, but after I don't know how many days of seeing elephants and monsters coming out of the ceilings and walls, me being continually sick, feeling hot and cold at the same time, things are starting to get better. I have two fucking kids and I need to do this so I can see them again.'

'Sean son, you are a much stronger man than you think, fair play to you.'

Peter took the Voluntary Attendance Form booklet again, and drew a small arrow pointing to the line where Sean needed to sign to confirm that the interview was over and that no further action would be taken against him. He handed Sean the pen but his attempt at applying a signature was even more erratic than the last. Peter again retrieved the pen from Sean's

hand.

'Boy Sean, you really got to get the shakes sorted out.'

'That's nothing; I used to have to keep a tie in the flat when I was on the booze.'

Peter recalled the wardrobe with one door hanging off, a coffee table and little else. This

was not the sort of pied a terre where one would have expected to see a collection of

gentleman's ties. Furthermore, Sean did not look like someone who had ever worn a tie.

'What on earth did you need a tie for, important guests or what?'

'Give me yours and I'll show you.'

Peter reluctantly removed his tie and handed it to Sean, hoping it would not make contact

with the vomit stains on the front of his shirt. Sean tied one end of the tie around his left

wrist, draped the tie around the back of his neck, grabbing the other end of the tie with his

right hand.

'I used to put the vodka glass in my left hand and drag it to my mouth like this,' Sean said as

he pulled the tie with his right hand. 'If I didn't do that I would spill more than I drank.'

Peter glanced quickly at Des, long enough to see that his face had frozen in utter disbelief.

Des completed the necessary details on the Voluntary Attendance Form while Peter led

Sean to the Enquiry Office and exit door. He could see Peter remove his wallet from his suit

pocket and hand Sean a ten pound note before he left to return to Artillery House.

CHAPTER NINE – A RABBIT APPEARS

Des had settled well into the irregular and at times irrational workings of North Queen Street C.I.D. office, it's characters, anomalies, but most of all the not knowing what each day will bring. An eight hour shift ceased to be the norm.

He still adored his BMW Z4, it certainly caught admiring glances, particularly during the rare summer days when he could electronically peel back the roof. Admiration of the car by females unfortunately never extended to its driver. For Des, 'Babe Magnet' was an additional extra that never came with his car. He took care each day to park it in an area of the bullet pockmarked station yard where he thought it least likely to suffer attack by shooting or a petrol bomb being lobbed over the station walls.

One early morning, after he and Peter had managed to extract themselves from Bob's tales of folklore detective stories in the tea room, it was noticed that Des had left his car keys on the heavily stained formica coffee table. Bob, with the body of a man 20 years older than he was, had a boy like humour of someone 50 years younger. Suddenly the kernel of an idea was born in Bob's mind.

Parking within the station yard was especially cramped and it was not uncommon for cars parked in lined parking bays to be hemmed in by impatient drivers abandoning their cars. Senior Officers and permanent operational office staff had clearly demarcated parking bays at the front of the main station entrance door, clearly stating their ranks and warnings not to park therein. Some considered the invasion of their clearly marked parking space as a heinous crime, to be investigated with stealth and utter determination in order to identify the miscreant, ignoring the realities of life just outside of the heavily fortified station walls.

Bob, addressing no one in particular in the tea room, picked up the keys and said, 'Say fuck all, if he comes looking for them deny seeing them, back soon.'

Employing the same zeal and energy Bob had used in deliberately avoiding work during his C.I.D. career, he eventually found a locksmith that would be able to copy the keys for Des's BMW Z4. Task completed, a feeling of smug satisfaction and a job well done, he rewarded himself with a few pints of Guinness in the Kitchen Bar in the city centre before returning to the C.I.D. office in time for lunch. Des later retrieved his keys from the coffee table, unaware of the journey they had taken.

Des had adopted Peter's habit of arriving early for their shift in the mornings, partly to avoid commuter traffic and partly to ensure a decent parking place was available. Des parked at the rear of the station, an area he favoured as it was well protected and he was less likely to be hemmed in by other vehicles. He walked away from his car, gleaming radiantly from a recent expensive wax and polish, (the car, not Des), and pressed the lock on his key, smiling in appreciation as the locks thudded shut and the indicators flashed in acknowledgement. Parking where he did meant a longer walk to the station entrance, but he considered the exertion worthwhile. Des loved his mum and his car more than anything.

As a veteran of almost two weeks in North Queen Street C.I.D., and with the help of Peter's advice, Des no longer feared the morning ritual in the tea room, though still tried to avoid direct contact with Bob, who unnoticed by most present, disappeared mid-sentence this morning when Des started to make himself and Peter a coffee. As he sat down amidst the rest of Bob's audience Bob reappeared and continued where he had left off, interrupting several other conversations, as if he had never left the room.

The offensiveness of Bob's exhortations about present day policewomen being, 'unshaggable bloody feminists,' and unable to take a good drink, or tell a good lie under oath were interrupted by the station tannoy.

'Acting Detective Constable O'Dowd contact the Enquiry Office immediately.'

'Fucking Blackey again,' Peter said as he dialled the Enquiry Office.

'It takes the same effort to phone as to tannoy, I asked you politely to phone the next fucking time.'

'Busy, fuck off and put Des on.'

Those in the tea room could only hear Des's conversation on the phone, witnessing the fact that Des was becoming somewhat more assertive.

'No it's not me, I parked at the back of the station.'

'I'm telling you Blackey, it's not me, and I do know exactly where I parked.'

'No I did not park in the Chief Inspectors bay. Yes I know that is at the front of the station and clearly marked, and that is why I would never park there.'

'Yes I do own a silver BMW Z4, what's the registration you got.'

'Yes that is mine, but it's not where you say it is parked for fuck sake.'

'Okay I will look out of the window, give me a second.'

Des had to climb onto an office desk in order to look out of a purposefully small, rocket and blast proof office window.

'Fuck how did that get there.'

'No I do not know any fucking magicians, I will move it now.'

As Des rushed downstairs to the car park, the rest of the C.I.D. office staff now aware of Bob's prank looked down from the windows to see Des strutting back and forth from the area where he had in fact parked his car to the Chief Inspectors bay where it now illegally sat, locked and secured. He was looking back and forth repeatedly, trying to consolidate in his own mind his actions when he drove his car into North Queen Street Station only ten minutes earlier.

Des's removal of his vehicle from the Chief Inspectors bay was simultaneous with the distribution of an internal station memorandum to all staff reminding them to respect and obey restrictions on using senior staff parking bays under threat of disciplinary action if violated. Whilst the handful of senior officers and staff parking bay holders felt a sense of inferiority, and cosy warmth and security by the issuance of the memorandum, the rest of the station personnel laughed and openly ridiculed its content. Des had unwittingly become a cause celebre and very soon ceased explaining the real version of where he had indeed parked his car, but stopped short of falsely admitting that he intentionally parked in the revered and hallowed space of the Chief Inspector.

Even Bob realised, after the veiled warnings the other Detectives in the office conveyed, that yes everyone had found it funny, but a repeat performance was out of the question given the incommensurate response by the hierarchy. What Bob failed to mention was that he had hidden a vibrator, an Ann Summers rampant rabbit to be precise (used, and source never revealed), in between the passenger sun visor and roof of the BMW Z4.

About two weeks after the mysterious station car park incident, Des had taken his mother to St Georges Market in Belfast. The weather was as best as you could expect for a Northern Ireland summer so Des wound back the sun roof as his mother put down the sun visor to avoid the glare of the mid-morning sun. As she did so the battery powered rampant rabbit fell onto her lap, triggering the on switch as it did so, sending it floundering around the passenger foot well like a line caught salmon just landed upon a small fishing boat. Des stopped the car immediately and reached down and grabbed the phallic writhing object that in no way resembled a cute bunny, and managed to switch off the power supply, rendering it rather pathetic.

'Sorry Mum, I promise I have no idea how that got there, I will chuck it into a bin at the market.'

Des's mum desperately grabbed the rampant rabbit from his grasp.

'No, it's okay son, a woman knows best how to get rid of those nasty things,' and she carefully nursed it into her commodious handbag.

Bob never told anyone about planting the rampant rabbit. Des never told anyone about the rampant rabbit falling on his mother's lap from the sun visor. Des's mother never told anyone that she had given the orphan rabbit a good home.

CHAPTER TEN – DOMESTIC DISTURBANCE

It was 10.55 pm and Sergeant Alison Reid was waiting on the rest of C Section to attend the briefing room before she commenced her intelligence updates, list of wanted persons/vehicles in the station area, and assignment of specific duties. No one enjoyed night duty. Seven continuous nights working from 11pm to 7am. Home to bed around 8am and a limited fitful sleep for most until around midday. Others, the more fortunate few, could sleep until late afternoon and beyond. Others, even fewer in number, would go home and whenever spouses and children vacated the house would enjoy their favourite alcoholic tipple, until feeling quite tipsy and staggering to bed, waking up in familiar enough surroundings, but not knowing if it was night or day, the realisation that another night duty dawned crushing their desire to get out of bed, but increasing their desire to have another quick drink before heading to work.

Gus was the last to enter the Briefing Room, chewing gum, grinning from ear to ear, whilst the rest of C Section sat around rather morosely, their faces and body language displaying the effects of sleep deprivation and intolerance. Alison knew from experience that Gus fitted the last category of post night duty sleepers and never assigned him driving duties on night shifts.

Alison detailed Ronnie as Station Duty Officer as always. 2 Part Time Reserve Constables paraded for duty. The Part Time Reserve force consisted of civilians with day jobs who gave up their time voluntarily, and for very little financial recompense, in order to assist and bolster the sometimes stretched resources of the Regular and Full Time Reserve personnel. They normally worked one or two duties each month, but it was rare that any volunteered for night duties. A lot of full time police officers questioned their motives for this selfless devotion. Others simply did not care, and welcomed the additional manpower, others considered them a bloody nuisance and a drain on manpower, as they had to be looked after.

Alison had no problem with her Part Time Reserve Constables Edna and Eric, whom she had employed many times at Carrickfergus Police Station. Both were 7th Day Adventists,

Edna lived in nearby Larne and Eric just a short journey further north in Ballygally. Both were married and had grown up children. Edna was five four inches tall, with a thin frame that bore the weight of Kevlar plated body armour with some difficulty. Her face was mouse like, her skin pale enough to appear as if she was allergic to the sun, and she was shy in conversation. Eric was smaller, but with the demeanour of someone eighteen inches taller and five stones heavier. He had balding ginger hair and an unremarkable face except for the randomly sprouting hairs between his upper lip and nose that he had tried for most of his adult life to cultivate into a moustache. Eric spoke with the booming voice and confidence of a man he would like to have been. Edna and Eric were lovers and had joined the Part Time Reserve Force for no other reason than to be in each other's company and procreate as often as possible during an eight hour period of duty. Most police officers with whom they worked were aware of this.

'Edna and Eric, nice to see you back again, many thanks. Sangar security duties for you both if that's okay,' Alison said, smiling.

Edna looked at the floor, her face reddening.

'Thank you Sergeant,' boomed Eric, jutting out his 34 inch chest. 'We will not let you down.'

'Two wee lovebirds in a sangar together, doesn't get any more romantic than that,' Gus interjected. No one flinched, the truth for them was that this was as romantic as they could get, and no one else really cared.

Sergeant Reid detailed the first response vehicle crew Delta 50, and then Gus and Tony Stockman as second response vehicle Delta 51, Tony as driver, Gus as Observer. Alison had learned that they had had a slight falling out over the recent suicide and thought it a good idea to team them together and try to restore harmony.

'Okay everyone know what they are doing?' she asked rhetorically, 'break time from 0200hr until 0400hr, sleep or watch the latest Bruce Willis movie in the TV room.'

Police Regulation break times should be for 45 minutes only and staggered so that there was always a vehicle on patrol. Sergeant Reid, and many of her ilk adopted a more flexible approach on night shift. Even Superintendent Brett Mayne would not pay a surprise visit in the middle of the night. But she knew she could rely on Eric and Edna for any quick alert, and that they would not inform anyone of the night shift break arrangements, and they in turn knew that their affair remained entirely confidential.

Ronnie locked up the armoury adjacent to the Station Enquiry Office after signing out radios and body armour to each officer, and Heckler and Koch MP5 machine guns to the two observers and Eric.

'You ready for a cup of tea Alison,' he shouted down the corridor to the Sergeants office.

'Yes, what's taken you so long?'

'Been busy dealing with the gladiators and foot soldiers your Empress.'

Alison only drank Earl Grey tea, with milk and two heaped spoonsful of sugar that were sure to detract from the unique flavour of the tea. Ronnie drank strong black tea that left marks and staining that would easily destroy delicate china cups. He used instead a seemingly indestructible army issue multi use drinking vessel that he had inherited from his days as Royal Ulster Constabulary Liaison Officer with locally garrisoned military personnel – now all returned to British or foreign soils. He never dwelled on the other uses for which the vessel had been put to use.

He brought in the teas and slumped down on the chair nearest to Alison's desk.

'Only one more night to go Ronnie, and then long weekend off.'

'Funny, I just about get into a night shift routine and then it finishes,' Ronnie sighed.

'For nearly 30 years, on and off, I could never, and will never settle into a night shift.'

'You happy with Gus and Tony together Alison, we don't need an incident with them drawing unwanted attention our way.'

'They'll be fine. Tony has a bit of a chip on his shoulder about never being accepted for the Regular Force despite the strongest recommendations. To make matters worse they send Gus to our Section, who was only able to join the force, and pass rather hurriedly through Police College because of his footballing ability. I think the two of them will gel.'

'Can't wait to see that mutual appreciation society take off, but I do as always defer to your seniority, knowledge, people handling and communication skills.'

'I have known you too long to know that you have never deferred to police seniority in your career, and never likely to change.'

'That's a fair point Alison, a bit insensitive but I'll get over it.'

'If I were to offer you a wee Bushmills malt while the boys are watching the movie would that help you get over it?'

'Always know how to sweet talk me don't you. See you here 2ish,' Ronnie replied as he rose wearily from the chair to make his way back to the Station Enquiry Office.

'Before you go Ronnie, have a look at this crap,' Alison said as she threw a report from the Divisional Commander onto his lap.

The subject heading was 'Holes in the footpath and roadways of our Division,' and was addressed to all supervisory uniform ranks and read as follows;

'Last month in a central London borough a pensioner returning home on foot from his local pub fell into an excavation pit on the footpath that was clearly unlit and did not meet the satisfactory health and safety requirements in terms of warnings and sufficient barriers and cone placements. Upon receipt of this information, and out of my concern for the welfare of all our Divisional residents I personally undertook a random but thorough reconnaissance of many of our roads, major and minor, and was shocked by the potential for similar catastrophes occurring within D Division. We are servants to the public and it is our function above all else to ensure their wellbeing. It is incumbent upon all uniform supervisors to ensure that their personnel are aware of this, and to initiate a reporting procedure whereby all holes in the road/footpath are identified and reported through the necessary channels for immediate attention. I implore you to include local residents in this initiative, through our officers or by direct contact with me, as I know residents in some areas (Carrickfergus for example), have little faith in local policing. This is such an important personal issue for me, and I wish to be kept fully informed.' Signed Brett Mayne, Superintendent, Divisional Commander.

'I see that the stuttering Napoleon has copied the report to the Chief Constables office, that's why it is such an important issue for him,' Ronnie sighed, 'unless of course his own father met his demise in such a way, and if he did he probably threw himself in.'

'Read into it Ali, a drunk walking home and staggering at angles from one footpath to the other wouldn't be aware of any obstacles even if they had been illuminated by Blackpool City Council. And of course, he had to mention bloody Carrickfergus, bring us under the spotlight yet again without foundation, a malicious stuttering bloody dwarf.'

'I agree, that angers me, and that's why I leave it to you to make some sort of response – not traceable back to Carrickfergus Police Station of course,' Ali replied and winked conspiratorially.

'Leave it to me Ali, he still doesn't know who put the dog shit through his letter box, we will be avenged by the time the top is taken off the bottle of Bush.'

Carrickfergus Police Station, no different to others, had security sangars at the front and rear of the station while CCTV monitored the side walls and fed into screens at the front (main) sangar. Normal duties involved both sangars being manned and personnel rotated from one to the other every hour, with meal break coverage being provided by other personnel. It was vital but tedious work, and only the most disciplined would be unable to nod off during night duties. The sangars were generally dirty, smelly, and semen stained with graffiti on the walls that unlike cuneiform needed no expert interpretation. Despite the aforesaid duty rules, everyone on C Section Night Duty knew that Eric and Edna shared the front sangar, ignored the rear sangar, and never emerged for meal breaks. This allowed Allson some flexibility in manpower, and allowed Eric and Edna maximum time together.

Not wishing to enter the front sangar personally and indiscreetly less he should provoke an attack of coitus interruptus Ronnie used the tannoy to ask Eric to attend the Enquiry Office. The sangar was barely larger than a good-sized garden shed but it took Eric an unseemly and guilt proving length of time to respond, and acknowledge he was making his way to meet Ronnie at the Enquiry Office.

'What do you think it is Eric,' Edna enquired.

'Special duties Edna, won't be the first time I've been asked to step up.'

'Oooo Eric, remember the last time, you were gone for over an hour and couldn't tell me what you had done.'

'Yes of course, but that's the way of special ops Edna.'

Eric walked towards the Enquiry Office, body armour and Heckler and Koch MP5 machine gun in hand, against a moonlight that Edna thought reminiscent of Clint Eastwood in western movies that she could not remember the name of.

'Hi Ronnie, what can I do for you.'

'Eric, do you remember the time recently when the Divisional Commander sent out a report about excessive dog shit on the pavements in the Division and we took you near to his house on night duty and you bravely poured a box of dog shit through his letter box.'

'Not really Ronnie, because you told me to erase the whole thing from my mind.'

'Okay, let's say then that you dreamt it.'

'But I didn't Ronnie.'

'Okay it didn't happen, that's fine. What I want you to do now is read the following sentence, assure me you understand it, rehearse it, and then you are going to say it down the phone when I tell you, without interruption or pause, then I will hang up

After several Hollywood attempts to give stage presence to the sentence, and dummy rehearsals, Ronnie finally had Eric ready to make his phone debut.

It was just before 2am and Ronnie rang Superintendent Brett Mayne's mobile number from an external police connection that would come up as number unknown. He answered almost immediately after the first ring as it was habit for him to keep the phone on his pillow.

'Is that Mr Mayne,' Eric bellowed in an uncannily deep masculine voice.

'This is Su, Su, Superintendent Mayne.'

'The same man, I just wanted to let you know I am an insomniac and street walker and only now have seen several holes in the roads and footpaths in the Newtownabbey area that I feel I should report to you directly as I don't trust tho boat officers. Ballyclare Road, Belfast Road, Shore Road, Greenisland Road, Rathcoole Street, Rathmore Avenue, Rathmore Crescent, Abbey Avenue, Enniskillen Road, Aboyne Avenue, Carrickfergus Road………..

Brett Mayne hung up the phone and swore that he would eventually find out who was to blame for this assassination of his most recent promotion seeking initiative, he knew he should have never encouraged public participation. C Section Carrickfergus were not even considered as potential perpetrators - yet.

'Excellent Eric, a job well done, and what a deep and manly voice if you don't mind me saying.'

'I raise my game when the situation calls for it Ronnie.'

'You shall now be hailed as Eric Invicta.'

'Mmm, just Eric is fine, can I head back now Ronnie.'

'You can, and to a hero's welcome, only keep this between us, Edna doesn't have to know the detail, does she?'

'She knows not to ask in these circumstances Ronnie.'

At around 0130hr, just as Eric completed his phone call to Superintendent Mayne, Delta 50 the first response vehicle attended a vehicle theft and Delta 51, Tony and Gus were sent to a domestic disturbance at a house in the Castlemara estate. Castlemara was never likely to feature in a Britain in Bloom competition, most of its open spaces and greenery still cluttered with the shells of burned out vehicles and the remains of celebratory bonfires in the name of William of Orange. The lung poisoning odour from thousands of burned out tyres still permeated.

There had been little but perfunctory conversation between Gus and Tony, with Gus fighting sleep as the alcohol filtered from his system.

'What number did uniform give out Gus?'

'48, the names Johnson, think I have been here before, she always backs down and never makes a statement. He is an arsehole.'

Number 48 was in the middle of a long row of fairly modern terraced housing. Every house without fail had a flagpole attached to the wall, flying either the Union Jack, Ulster Flag or Ulster Defence Association flag. Failure to display a flag meant a visit from local UDA 'volunteers' who didn't call round for tea and biscuits and a friendly chat.

Numbers 46 and 50 had their livingroom lights on but with curtains shut, not wishing to reveal themselves as potential witnesses, as cooperation with the police was also forbidden by the 'volunteers,' no matter how dire the circumstances.

'Do you want me to call for back up Tony.'

'Nah, we are okay.'

'You take him and I'll take her.'

'Fine.'

It was unwritten procedure for officers attending a domestic disturbance to initially separate the factions, preferably into different rooms, and make reasonable assessments as to each other's state of mind and allegations without a shouting match intervening between them. The small square of glass in the front door was smashed and the door was lying open. A male voice could be heard screaming and threatening above the crying of a female voice. Gus knocked loudly on the open door.

'Fuck off you black bastards, she didn't mean to call you, she's just had a wee bit too much to drink, now fuck off.'

Her screaming, indecipherable, became louder when she realised the police had arrived. Gus and Tony walked uninvited down the short hallway and into the living room. Furniture had been overturned and the television screen smashed. There was an overpowering odour of stale alcohol, and empty bottles of cheap cider littered the bare remnants of the carpet.

There she was cowering and squat between the living room window and the corner of the settee; natures flight instinct and self-preservation had drawn her to the smallest area her emaciated frame could fit, an area that made it almost impossible for punches and kicks to rein in on her with any real force. He sat proudly on the settee drinking from a bottle of cider.

'I told you to fuck off, you need a fucking warrant to be in here.'

'Bloody hell Tony, we are dealing with an expert in law here.'

'Looks just like a useless wife beating dickhead to me.'

Mr Johnson made to rise from the settee and was pushed back down by Tony without any resistance, happy to continue drinking his cider.

Gus bent down, brought Mrs Johnson to her feet, and walked with her to the kitchen. She had bruises on her cheek and right eye and was bleeding slightly from her nose.

'Do you want me to call an ambulance Mrs Johnson.'

'No I'm fine, really. You got here before he really started on me,' she gasped through heaving and sobbing.

'Take a seat at the table, try and calm down a bit, he's not going to hit you anymore. I'll get you a glass of water.'

Gus handed over the water, and it was a struggle for her to stop spilling the entire contents as her hands shook so badly on grasping the glass.

'I think I have been here before Mrs Johnson.'

'The whole of Carrickfergus station have been here over the years I'm sure,' she replied, the sobbing easing slightly, and breathing trying desperately to return to normal.

'Didn't I arrange for you to meet with the Domestic Violence Officer.'

'He said he would beat the shit out of me if I did,' she said, feeling the bruising and swelling on her cheek and eye.

'Then why do you keep on letting him away with this. It's never going to stop until you take positive action against him. Given the history, we can have a restraining order on him that will stop him coming anywhere near you or the house.'

'That won't stop him. If he can't get near me he will send his family.'

'Then we will deal with them as well.'

'Constable you can't be here all the time – me, I have nowhere else to go.'

'You've no kids have you?'

'No, and praise the bloody lord for that.'

'Are you going to make a complaint this time, once and for all put a stop to this.'

'No Constable, just put him out. He'll go around to his mates in Rathcoole for drink and crash out there.'

'And what about tomorrow.'

'He'll promise never to do it again and be okay for a wee while.'

'Until the next time.'

'Aye.'

Tony took a cursory glance around the living room. It was grim but not squalid. It was evident that Mrs Johnson made an attempt at good housekeeping with what little decent items of household furnishings she had. Above the fireplace hung a framed photograph of Michael Stone taken inside the Maze Prison. Stone had earned loyalist paramilitary hero status when high on drugs, and drunk from the alcohol he had drunk through the night in an illegal drinking club. Thus, his senses dulled to say the least, he had found the courage to attack mourners at an Irish Republican Army funeral at Milltown Cemetery in West Belfast. He lobbed hand grenades and fired shots at the hundreds in attendance, killing three and injuring over fifty. In sobriety, the death count would have been much higher. He was chased and caught by a crowd of mourners and would surely have been beaten to death had police not arrived on the scene as quickly as they did and rescued him. Tony shared the view, like the majority of police officers, that police in attendance should have reacted much more slowly to the attack being inflicted upon Stone. Also adorning the walls were the customary 'No Surrender' prints and homages to William of Orange.

'Mr Johnson, do you have a first name?'

'Yes, its fuckin Sir to you.'

'Mr Johnson, why do you feel it necessary to hit your wife.'

'Haven't touched her, you ask her. She tripped and fell and hurt herself, end of, now fuck off out of my house.'

'Where exactly did she trip and fall.'

'Fuck do I know, ask her.'

'Mr Johnson, would it be fair to say that you are just a low life scumbag.'

Gus had left Mrs Johnson in the kitchen, the door closed behind him, and walked into the living room just in time to see Mr Johnson rise from the settee and stumble drunkenly towards Tony. Tony drew back his right arm and with an open palm slapped Mr Johnson fiercely across the side of his face, causing him to fall fully lengthways across the settee. The noise of the slap was painful and unforgettable. Mr Johnson held both his hands to his cheek in the vain attempt that it may lessen the excruciating tingling pain he was experiencing. Tony then punched Mr Johnson in the testicles, causing him to immediately remove his hands from his cheek to try and administer comfort to a much more intense pain.

'The slap mark will be gone in a few minutes; you have the choice now. I arrest you for Assault on a Police Officer or we take you out of here, drop you off well away from here, and you stay away until tomorrow. What do you want.'

Mr Johnson was unable to respond coherently as he shifted his hands to and fro his stung cheek and his testicles.

'Sorry Mr Johnson, what did you say.'

'I'll fucking go.'

Gus and Tony deposited a forlorn and contrite Mr Johnson at his friend's house in the Rathcoole estate some miles away from Carrickfergus.

Gus turned to Tony, offered the palm of his hand and said, 'High five.' Tony, a bit bemused, responded and as they exchanged high fives Gus said, 'Great skills mate, respect, total respect.'

'Thanks Gus.'

At 2am precisely Ronnie settled into the chair beside Alison's desk, a far from paltry glass of Bushmills Malt in his hand, and saw Gus and Tony walk past on their way to the TV room, chatting and laughing together like long-time friends recently reunited.

'I don't know how, but you can do it Ali.'

'That's why I am a supervisor Ronnie.'

'Bollocks Sergeant.'

CHAPTER ELEVEN – BEDSIT BURGLARY

It was approaching 10.30pm and Pete and Des were sitting with their feet up watching television in the relative comforts of the rest room/tea room/unofficial bar in the North Queen Street C.I.D. office. The stress cupboard had just been opened and Des nursed a glass of martini while Pete listened to the clink of the ice in his gin and tonic as he swirled the contents around in order to savour the aroma; enjoying delaying the delight of having his first sip. Having started work at 8am it was time to wind down on the approach to the end of duty at midnight, inwardly praying that no further incidents would occur requiring their attendance.

At the same time Peter Martin, a 70-year-old former homeless alcoholic had just retired to his bed, a settee on which he slept fully clothed with a blanket covering him in his barely habitable ground floor bedsit at 16a Duncairn Gardens. He had a 3 bar electric fire for heating which he used summer and winter. When he went to bed he kept one bar on throughout the night. Underwear, shirts and socks were trying with some difficulty to dry as they hung from a piece of string that stretched from above the entrance door to the toilet door.

He had earlier been watching television on a portable black and white television set given to him by a local charity, testament to the durability of 1970s technology. There was a small electric cooker in the room, and a separate toilet with electric shower.

Duncairn Gardens, separated the staunchly republican neighbourhood of the New Lodge from the loyalist Tigers Bay, and had seen far better days. A once much sought after salubrious area of three and four storey Victorian houses, the 'Troubles' rendered it a battleground for the protestant and catholic neighbours on either side. Residents fled their elegant homes, those that survived the carnage and destruction eventually being turned into flats and bedsits for those considered undesirable to obtain accommodation elsewhere. There was a mix of former and current alcoholics, drug addicts, prostitutes, pimps, mentally unstable, and those just wanting to get on with their lives. This was not bohemian chic.

At about 11pm, callsigns Delta 70 and 71, a two vehicle police patrol in armoured landrovers spotted a male person walking up Duncairn Gardens towards Antrim Road. He struggled to carry a portable television under one arm, shifting it from left to right to try and gain the best hold. The lead vehicle of the two stopped beside the man and the observer in the front passenger seat swung open the heavy armoured door, leaned out and asked where he had got the television from.

'I found it.'

'Where?'

'Just on the street back there.'

'Not the sort of street I thought was paved in television sets.'

'What you on about, why do you pick on me; because I am gay? Why can't you leave me fucking alone?'

'Because you are carrying a television set under your arm late at night, not because you are gay, how would I know you were gay.'

'All the city centre police knows me, they know I am gay and proud to shout it out man, you knows what I mean dude.'

He tried to affect the mannerisms of a gangster rappa in a most ineffectual way

His name was Gerry Dalzell and he lived in an equally undesirable area on the Antrim Road. He was making his way home on foot after spending most of the day drinking cider and Bucksfast with a group of gay friend's at the city centre bandstand at Cornmarket, and just happened to find the television set on his way home.

The police officers looked at the television. By its age and appearance, it was quite likely someone may have thrown it out, but not in this neighbourhood.

'Delta 70, 70 from uniform.'

'Uniform from Delta 70 send over.'

'Delta 70 could you attend 16a Duncairn Gardens, fire service and ambulance still in attendance, report of a burglary and arson with intent to endanger life.'

'Uniform from Delta 70, anything reported stolen from this address.'

'Delta 70, just an old portable television.'

'Uniform from Delta 70 roger, get back to you as soon as possible.'

'Gerry you are arrested,' and he was lead into the rear of the armoured landrover beside the third police crew member who closed the heavy double doors behind them. Gerry started to cry, but not real tears, and was ignored.

On attendance at 16a Duncairn Gardens, Peter Martin was still being attended to in the back of an ambulance. The fire service unit commander took the police observer into the bedsit and explained his findings as the police surveyed the scene. The front and only window to the bedsit was fully open, its lock long rusted away. In the middle of the bedsit lay a pile of burned and smouldering clothing, in a circular shape, around the remains of an electric fire. Pieces of burned string could be made out amongst the debris. The walls and ceiling were damaged by smoke. The settee had been almost destroyed by fire. The fire service unit had been returning from a call to its base at Antrim Road and saw the smoke coming from the bedsit as they drove past, otherwise the blaze would have consumed the bedsit and anyone in it.

Peter was sitting upright in the back of the ambulance, his face, hair and clothes blackened by the acrid smoke that emanated from the settee. He had no trousers on and there were superficial burn marks to his legs and the jumper he was wearing. He was receiving oxygen from a face mask and at the same time declining any offers by the paramedics to take him to the nearby Mater Hospital for a check-up. He seemed unperturbed by the whole incident, as if it was just part of daily routine. Clearly this response could mask the onset of shock and the paramedics finally persuaded him by reminding him that he had nowhere else to go, no bathing facilities to remove the pervading smell of smoke that clogs the pores of the skin and any clothing being worn, and had no clothes to change into. Delta 70 observer was allowed to speak to him briefly before he was taken to the Mater Hospital.

It emerged that Peter had been woken from his sleep by a man who had entered the bedsit through the front window. The man smelled strongly of alcohol, grabbed Peter by the throat, and demanded that he hand over all his money and jewellery. He was thin like Peter, but half his age, and possessed a strength Peter could no longer match.

'I don't have any jewellery,' Peter had answered, still drowsy.

'Where's the money.'

'I have about two pounds in my pocket, here take it,' as he fumbled to try and remove the coinage, struggling against the hold on his throat.

'Where's the fucking rest.'

'Look around you, it's not a fucking palace, this is all I have.'

'Funny fucker eh, we'll soon see.'

The man dragged Peter to his feet, forced him to bend over the cooker face downwards, and pulled down Peter's trousers and underpants. Peter had felt a tinge of embarrassment at the possible state of his underpants. The man started to fondle Peter's penis from behind. The man then unzipped his trousers and tried for several minutes to forcibly insert his penis into Peter's anus while simultaneously holding onto Peter's penis. Peter tried to free himself but found himself powerless.

Unable to gain a sustainable erection the intruder forced Peter to sit on the floor and snatched the clothes string and contents from above him. He tied Peter's hands and feet with the string and placed the electric heater so close to him he could feel the intense heat on his skin almost immediately. He then gathered and threw the drying clothes, and others lying nearby on top of the heater and around Peter. This had the soothing and temporary effect of removing the pain caused by the direct contact with the fire and his skin, to be revisited when the clothes slowly ignited around him.

The man looked around quickly for anything of value he could steal and settled on the portable black and white television. He picked it up and left via the front door, an exit made easier due to Peter's habit of leaving the key in the lock at nights. As soon as Peter heard the heavy main front door to the bedsits being slammed closed he began screaming, and writhing in an attempt to free himself from the ties around his ankles and wrists.

Luckily many of the clothing items surrounding him were not completely dry and slow to fully ignite, but he could feel the pain of burning in several areas on his legs. He could see that the drier clothes next to the settee had already ignited the fabric and whilst relatively flameless the black smoke was filling the room very quickly and he was struggling to breathe. After what seemed like an eternity but was in fact a matter of minutes, a fireman appeared at his open window, almost ghost like through the dense smoke. Peter did not believe in god, but he did feel a prayer had been answered.

He was shown a portable black and white television set by a police officer and identified it as his own. The police told Peter a Detective would obtain a full statement from him after he had been admitted to and treated at the Mater Hospital.

'Uniform from Delta 70 over.'

'Delta 70 from Uniform send over.'

'Uniform from Delta 70, one male person arrested for Burglary and Arson to Endanger Life and will be taken to Antrim Road Custody suite. Request C.I.D. and Scenes of Crime to 16a Duncairn Gardens. Delta 71 remaining to secure the scene.'

'Delta 70 from Uniform roger, will do. Give me the arrested persons details by landline from the Custody Suite.'

'Uniform from Delta 70, roger that.'

The phone rang in the C.I.D. rest room. Peter looked at the phone, and at his watch, reluctant at first to answer. He picked it up and Des watched and listened to Peter's side of the two-way conversation.

'Ah for fucks sake.'

'Yes, understand all that, nah can't pass that onto Night Duty, we will go.'

'No its okay, tell Delta 71 we will take a race up in the armoured C.I.D. car and see them at the scene before we go to the Mater Hospital. We will need cover at the hospital, give you a time later.'

Peter told Des to put the recently poured drinks into the fridge and explained the background to the scene they were now about to attend. It was 1am by the time they had finished the scene examination and taken a statement from the victim at the Mater Hospital. They had now arrived at Antrim Road Custody suite to enquire if the suspect Gerry Dalzell was fit for interview, rather hoping that the Police Doctor who would have examined him upon his arrival may have recommended no interviews until the morning because of his alcohol consumption.

'Unlucky Pete, he's ready for interview as soon as his solicitor gets here,' Andy Moody the Custody Sergeant informed him.

'Who's he asked for?'

'Joe Dryden from Bogue and McNulty.'

Peter knew Joe well from interviews over the years and got on very well with him, occasionally bumping into him for a drink in the city centre. He could be combative but never intentionally obstructive or a hindrance. He had a job to do, regardless of his like or dislike of his client, and severity or distastefulness of the alleged crime. Peter appreciated this, many Detectives did not. There were many solicitors Peter didn't like and that feeling was openly reciprocated. He knew that Joe, like Peter at this time of the night, would just want a rapid conclusion, one way or the other.

'Did Joe say how long he was going to be?'

'He'll be here at half past.'

'Okay Andy, we'll be up the canteen having a coffee, give us a tannoy mate.'

At 1.35am, Peter and Joe were having an informal chat in the interview room while Des collected interview tapes and paperwork from the Custody office.

'Joe he fits the description, his clothes have been seized and I'm sure we'll get residue from the fire and smoke, and uniform police arrest him a short distance from the scene carrying the victim's television.' Peter purposefully did not reveal the content of Peter Martin's statement, or the conversation he had had with the arresting officer and his colleagues.

'Let me have a quick word with him before we start the interview Pete, I'll give you a nod when we're ready.'

Gerry Dalzell was escorted into the interview room by a member of the custody staff wearing a white prison boiler suit that came in XXL size only and served to make him appear diminutive.

The tape-recorded interview commenced at 1.45am. Peter introduced himself and Des, and added that Mr Dryden from Bogue and McNulty was present. He then asked Gerry to state his full name, date of birth and address which he did freely. Pete then reminded Gerry of the reason for his arrest and repeated the official police caution to him. Gerry acknowledged that he understood the caution after looking at his solicitor who nodded in agreement.

Peter had already told Des that this was a listen and learn interview that he would conduct in its entirety, and requested that Des simply take notes, and produce the portable television when requested to present it in evidence when shown to Gerry Dalzell. Des was more than happy with this arrangement.

'Gerry you were arrested at 11.10pm last night for the offences we have already mentioned, near the top of Duncairn Gardens by uniform police who saw you carrying a portable television set, isn't that right.'

'That is correct Detective,' Gerry replied, drawing out the word Detective for no particular reason.

'And a fucking liberty it was too,' Gerry added as an afterthought.

Joe Dryden nudged him and shook his head

'Sorry Detective, I get myself worked up, you know.'

'That's okay Gerry, if we just continue now. For the purposes of the tape Detective Constable O'Dowd is now showing you a portable television set labelled JM1. Is this the television set you were carrying when you were arrested last night?'

'I'm sure it is Detective.'

'Where did you get the television Gerry?'

'I found it on the street so I did.'

'It's not a great television Gerry but I would find it strange that it was simply left on the footpath.'

'This is Belfast Detective, I don't have to tell you the goings on here, know what I mean.'

'Gerry this television has been identified as having been stolen from a bedsit at 16a Duncairn Gardens only moments before you were arrested, and a very short distance from where you were arrested.'

'Oh my god Detective, if I had known that.'

'I believe that you broke into this bedsit Gerry.'

'Not on my bloody nelly.'

'Gerry are you homosexual.'

'Yes Detective, and anyone who knows me knows that. Loud and proud part of the gay community here, I've been in the papers.'

'Gerry the man who broke into this bedsit looking for money and jewellery forced the occupant over a cooker, hauled down his trousers and tried to bugger him. When he was unsuccessful he tied the occupant up with string, sat him on the floor, set an electric heater next to him and piled clothes around him and over the heater in a deliberate attempt to seriously injure or kill him. The television, JM1 already shown to you was stolen from the bedsit. You have admitted that you are a homosexual and in acceptance of that and the other evidence Gerry it leaves me in no doubt that you committed these offences.'

Peter, Des and Joe Dryden could not have prepared themselves for the immediate and indignant response.

'Well I have never been so bloody well insulted. Detective I want this on the tape to prove my innocence here, I am a receiver not a giver, a receiver not a bloody giver, honestly to god Detective you know you have the wrong man here.'

Joc looked at his client wide eyed in disbelief while trying to stifle laughter before turning to Peter and drawing his hand across his throat indicating a termination of the interview. Peter was gripping his leg, concentrating on the pain in order to stop a fit of laughter. Des stared unblinking at Gerry in bemused wonderment. The interview tapes were switched off and the paperwork concluded.

CHAPTER TWELVE – EMPTY ENVELOPES AND MORE

Superintendent Brett Mayne would describe himself, privately of course, as risk averse. A risk for Brett was to be avoided at all costs. Where there is risk in Brett's view there lurks the very distinct possibility of failure. Risk and failure were synonymous in Brett's mind. Brett's desire for promotion and return to Headquarters policing could easily be thwarted by any perceived failure on his part. For that reason, Brett chose early on his police career to never take risks. This was a path he stuck to rigorously.

This morning Brett Mayne took an impetuous and uncalculated risk.

After showering in his en suite bathroom, and before dressing, he fumbled through the collection of his nanny's thongs and g strings that he had amassed and hidden in the bottom of the drawer that contained his own underwear. He was convinced that only he knew of this illicit, increasing collection. The nanny knew and accepted this perversion but occasionally had to surreptitiously remove some of her own underwear as Brett was accumulating items quicker than she could buy them.

Brett held up one of his favourite thongs. Pure white, ornamentally laced, and a perfect fit for him when stretched. Brett impulsively threw aside his Marks and Spencer boxer shorts and pulled the thong as far up his crotch as was reasonably comfortable. He checked himself out in the mirror before dressing for work.

Brett entered Newtownabbey Police Station shortly after 8am and acknowledged the salutes and acts of homage as if he were a victorious gladiator who had just been give the thumbs up by a baying crowd. When he was out of sight he received fingers up in even greater numbers.

Brett sat at his desk, the stretch of the thong bringing unimaginable pleasure. This was a risk worth taking Brett thought to himself.

His office manager entered his office with open routine mail and a handful of unopened internal envelopes marked personally for the SDC, Newtownabbey. Brett cringed when he saw the personal internal envelopes.

'Brett the C.I.D. were trying to contact you, a catholic labourer has been shot dead on a building site at Rathcoole Drive and they have just left to go to the scene.'

'Ooh that's not so good. Tell them to keep me informed,' not for a moment averting his attention from the impending internal envelopes.

The Newtownabbey Station office manager was a spinster in her early sixties. She had secretly loved and adored all previous Sub Divisional Commanders she had worked for throughout her long career but disliked Brett.

'Coffee please Eileen, come come now, a bit on the slow side this morning aren't we,' Brett intoned, more buoyant and communicative than usual for this time of morning, or indeed any time of the day, and only he knew why. Christ this was a risk worth taking.

'I have devoted my life to this job Brett. I have never considered taking time off to attend juggling and balancing lessons at local council sponsored workshops, and I do feel it is rather late in my life to do it now. One of the office clerks will bring your coffee in a minute.'

'Thanks Eileen, you know the way I like it,' choosing to ignore the protest made by Eileen.

Eileen did know the way Brett liked his coffee but instructed her staff to make less than subtle variations every morning

Brett surveyed the two piles of mail in front of him. The larger contained the letters and reports that had been assembled by his office staff from routine incoming internal and external mail. The smaller contained envelopes of various sizes marked 'Personal For', that had arrived via the police internal mail courier system. The exterior front of the envelopes contained a grid of address boxes that allowed for multi-use within the system. Brett grimaced, but with his new-found confidence decided to tackle the ten to twelve internal envelopes first.

Brett had been in charge at Newtownabbey for two months now and accepted that his first few weeks were a difficult time for him in terms of settling in and adjustment. A time for his staff, police and civilian, to realise that he was the new brush sweeping clean the cobweb ridden past of the Royal Ulster Constabulary, without allowing them the time to adjust and resettle. Move forward or move out of the way was Brett's mantra, regardless of and insensitive to recent history and lost lives. He chose to be ignorant of the past lest it should affect shaping his future.

He took the first internal envelope from his desk, in beautifully formed hand written fountain pen ink, marked for the personal attention of the SDC Newtownabbey. Brett noticed from the previous addressee boxes that the envelope was well travelled, starting at Bangor Police Station, via various Belfast police stations, penultimately the Forensic Science Laboratory at Seapark, Carrickfergus, before reaching his desk at Newtownabbey Police Station. The handwriting was different throughout and he thought no doubt genuine. He opened the envelope and it was empty. He searched into each corner of the envelope – it was assuredly empty.

'Fuck,' he muttered to himself. In the last four to six weeks at least ninety per cent of his internal mail was empty. In the last seven working days, he had retained all the empty envelopes sent to him. By the time he had examined this morning's mail the total had reached sixty-three. It was time for action.

'Eileen, can you get the Chief Inspector C.I.D. to contact me as soon as possible please.'

'His number is on the contact sheet on your desk Brett.'

'Ah, so it is, what's his name.'

'Jim Duffy, you were supposed to attend the Chief Constables office when he got his Long Service Award last week.'

'I know but the Chief Constable was away and his deputy stood in.'

Eileen hung up before Brett could continue.

To Brett it was an inordinately long time before the Chief Inspector C.I.D. phoned his office in response to a message Brett left with the C.I.D. office manager. Brett tried as hard as he could to disguise his frustration.

'Chief Inspector could you come down to my office as soon as possible.'

'I just need to finish off debriefing my Detectives first, give me about fifteen minutes maximum.'

'Of course, of co, co, course, take your time,' Brett replied in astonishment. How were the C.I.D. so ahead of the game that they had already begun their investigation into the deluge of empty envelopes.

Jim Duffy had not yet met the new Sub Divisional Commander. He had heard enough negative reports that he did not feel the compunction to introduce himself until it was necessary in the course of his duties. Unfortunately for the Chief Inspector C.I.D. that time had come. Jim knocked on the S.D.C.'s door and was beckoned in immediately. Jim had been a more than regular visitor to this office during the tenure of the previous incumbent and was taken aback for a moment by the interior change. He stood by the desk, unsure whether to proffer a handshake, and thought the better of it and sat down. The Sub Divisional Commander made no attempt at introduction.

'Chief Inspector, I have asked you here personally, and in confidence, because this is a matter that will require the utmost secrecy.'

'Sir, the press have already been at the scene and are liaising with a Headquarters Press Officer for an official statement.'

'What, this has leaked already, what kind of station is this.'

'Sir, you can't hide the fatal shooting of a catholic workman on a protestant housing estate. Word spreads immediately.'

'You are not here for that Chief Inspector, as important as it is of course, a continuation of those so-called tit for tat shootings I am sure, never likely to end until we get this Police Service in order. I am here to brief you about the relentless empty envelope campaign that I have been a victim of, and how we proceed with lines of enquiry.' At that Brett threw the accumulated evidence onto his desk.

'This is where I suggest you start Chief Inspector,' outlining the empty envelope vendetta that had been waged against him.

'We investigate crime Sir, it's in the name,' Jim snarled, almost unable to contain his anger, 'no serious criminal offences have been committed.'

'So criminal damage to those envelopes is not a crime Chief Inspector.'

'Not sufficient for any level of investigation, never mind C.I.D.'

'Do I have to tell you your job Chief Inspector, hand writing analysis of those envelopes will identify a common denominator. Fingerprint analysis and D.N.A., similarly will identify one individual present on them all. This is an easy detection for the C.I.D.'

'We can only use these resources in the most serious of investigations, terrorist incidents and murders.'

'Well Chief Inspector, to further a meaningful relationship between us on a professional and personal level couldn't you piggy back this on your recent murder investigation.'

'I have four Detectives interviewing terrorists at Castlereagh Holding Centre, I sent my remaining Detectives to the murder scene at Rathcoole Drive and hope for additional resources from outside the region soon. I have sent a Detective to the mortuary with the remains of a young catholic labourer who was shot once in the chest and twice through the back of his head as he lay on the ground. There is nothing left of the front of his face apart from an eye and part of his left ear, and I have to meet with and explain this to his wife before she formally identifies what is left of him to the pathologist.'

'Well obviously, I appreciate that this is not a good time, but take the evidence with you and when time permits, hopefully in the next few days, you can provide me with an update. My D.N.A. and fingerprints are of course on record for elimination purposes.'

Chief Inspector C.I.D. collected the empty envelopes from the desk and left the S.D.C.s office without comment. Instead of walking along the adjoining corridors to the C.I.D. offices he diverted through an exit door near to the canteen and threw the envelopes into a skip marked 'For Burning Only'.

CHAPTER THIRTEEN – EARLY SHIFT AT CARRICFERGUS

'Good morning May, what specials are on this morning's menu.'

'Ah god in bloody heaven, C Section are back. Ronnie there are no specials, and there are no breakfast menus.'

'Then provide me with one of Compass Caterings Suggestion forms please May, immediate action needs to be taken.'

'Three weeks of fucking bliss and now you lot are back on earlies; it's going to be a long week.'

'My stomach aches for slightly smoked kipper, line caught from the bracing waters of Norway, cherry tomatoes, Italian of course, accompanied by a cheeky round of black pudding from award winning butchers in Stornoway in the wild north of Scotland.'

'You are im-fucking-possible Ronnie, why'd you talk that crap.'

'Because I lack the language skill that qualifies you to insert swear words into the middle of everyday words just to give them that edge.'

'Two full fries then Ronnie.'

'You win again May,' Ronnie stated out loud, just in time to see May smile as she turned to shout the order to Frank the cook.

Ronnie joined Ali at a table and both bemoaned how the off duty long weekend after their night duties had passed so quickly. Ali had put Gus and Tony together in Delta 50 the first response vehicle, Tony as driver and Gus as observer. Gus had to leave at 2pm for football training so Ali would replace him for the last hour of duty. The loss of Des on his three month secondment to C.I.D., and the long term sickness of a Woman Police Constable, who had appeared in Force Orders as transferred to Carrickfergus Police Station but never physically materialised. She had gone sick with work related stress on hearing of the transfer, depleting resources in such a way there was little room for interchange of manpower between the few positions that had to be detailed each shift. Importantly for Ali no one was complaining.

'How is Des getting on,' Ronnie asked, almost rhetorically.

'He was just coming good Ronnie and C.I.D. will open his eyes. No news is good news as far as I am concerned, and look forward to having the sleuth back.'

The telephone in the canteen rang and no one appeared to be willing to answer it. Ben and Joe the stations transport officer's elite were nearest to the telephone but seemingly deaf to its incessant ringing. They were still hurting from the witty, and some less witty remarks and jibes that came their way after finding 'brain matter' in the supervision vehicle. Eventually Joe nodded his head sideways towards the phone acknowledging its existence and Ben nodded his head down as if authorising him to answer it.

'Hello, Carrickfergus Motor Transport Officer, second in command here.'

'Hang on, I'll get him. Observer 50, its uniform,' Joe bellowed across the canteen, seeking a call sign rather than an individual.

Gus had just sat down with his breakfast and hauled himself up slowly from his seat. He sauntered across to the phone and explained not for the first time that radio connection in the canteen at Carrickfergus police station was poor at best. The control room operator, not for the first time, stated he would send a fault report to the technicians and outlined the details of a 999 call that had just been received at Police Headquarters.

Mrs Ivy Baird, a cleaning lady whose job it was to clean the King William the Third Memorial Orange Hall in Lancastrian Street one morning a week, before moving onto her six morning a week cleaning job at a nearby Bookmakers, reported that she had discovered what she had described as a 'big looking gun thing' in the shrubbery at the front of the hall.

'Suspicious object at the main Orange Hall Ali. Me and Tony will take a run up and let you know if there's anything doing.'

'Yeah, finish your breakfast,' Ali sighed, perfectly aware that Gus did not need an invitation to put his breakfast first in that clash of priorities.

The school runs hadn't yet started so traffic on the roads in Carrickfergus was light apart from the Marine Highway main road ferrying commuters into Belfast. Tony chose to avoid trying to join Marine Highway in a cityward direction and took a more circuitous route around the back of the police station, passing through small housing estates and thoroughfares before arriving at the Orange Hall at around 7.30am.

Gus radioed Belfast Regional Control to signify his arrival at the scene. He picked up his body armour from the rear seat of the vehicle, undecided for a moment whether he should wear it or not as he was uncomfortable after eating a large breakfast only moments earlier. He then slid it on and secured the velcro fastenings before approaching Mrs Baird who was standing alone at the open door of the orange hall. Tony left the driver's seat and stood at the front gate of the hall, overtly surveying traffic and pedestrians making their way up and down the street. Although protestant communities were generally regarded by police as less of a threat than nationalist communities, basic precautions were still taken.

'Well Mrs Baird, what have you gone and found for us today,' Gus asked, smiling at her as he would his own grandmother.

'Constable a bloody great gun is what it is. 'Mon I'll show you son.'

Mrs Baird walked the few short steps with Gus across the front grass area to some slightly overgrown shrubbery near to the front gate. Lain on the soil was a heavy-duty plastic liner on top of which appeared to be the double barrels of a shotgun, most of the stock and barrels covered in bricks, clearly visible from a short distance away. Gus knew that formal meetings in the hall and band practice occurred only two nights per week. The last being

138

three days ago according to Mrs Baird. He also knew that members visited the hall every evening to drink at the bar in contravention of the drinks licence they held. They were never rowdy or disturbed residents so no action was taken. It was unusual for any of the drinkers to remain beyond 10pm, and even the most visually impaired or drunk visitor could not have failed to notice the recent addition to the hall's horticulture. It was a very shoddy attempt at concealment and obviously recently placed.

Gus told Mrs Baird to go into the hall and go about her cleaning duties while he and Tony stooped over the reported suspect item.

'I think it's a shotgun Gus, dumped here in a hurry by the looks of it.'

'Mmm, can't quite see the whole of it yet to make sure.'

'Will I get bomb disposal to clear it Gus,' Tony asked as he walked back towards the police vehicle to retrieve his uniform hat, expecting a long wait in the street for the Ammunition Technical Officer team to arrive.

'Fuck, that means sealing off the whole bloody area for hours, hang on a second Tony.'

Gus stooped over what he firmly believed was a shotgun and carefully removed the bricks that had been concealing what he thought were the stock and most of the twin barrels. He was grinning in the knowledge that his original conclusion was correct as he removed the last brick.

The weight of the bricks had been holding down the arming lever of a home made grenade placed underneath the shotgun. The grenade was fitted with a zero delay fuse and had had it's pin removed. The small device had been filled with home made explosives and detonated immediately and with devastating effect. Hundreds of small shards of shrapnel from the device and shotgun barrels soared upwards and horizontally faster and as deadly as a bullet leaving a gun. The shrapnel that flew upwards was absorbed with some force by Gus's body armour. The shrapnel that escaped horizontally flew into Gus's right leg, as he

139

had been leaning to that side when removing the bricks. It ripped through his flesh and destroyed his tibia, fibula and kneecap. Only remnants of skin were left straining to keep his foot attached to the rest of his leg. His femur protruded through a gaping hole where his kneecap had been only a second earlier.

Gus was on the ground screaming in a way that Tony would never later be able to describe or forget. He was holding onto the lower portion of his protruding femur bone, searching downwards for the rest of his leg.

Tony radioed for immediate assistance, frenetic, hoping that his transmission was understood, and ran over to Gus. Where to start? Classroom first aid doesn't prepare you for this he thought frantically. Try and stem the blood loss and calm the patient – some fucking chance. The first aid kit in the police vehicle had nothing to deal with this, a few sticking plasters and sterile wipes, a fucking M.A.S.H. set up was needed here – weird thoughts running through his mind as he tried to think logically.

Tony ran into the Orange Hall just in time to prevent Mrs Baird from coming out and instinctively grabbed a white tablecloth, dislodging all sorts of Orange Order paraphernalia as he did so. He wrapped the tablecloth around Gus's leg as tight as he could, frightened that he might detach his foot from his leg in the process. He had his arm around Gus's shoulder trying to calm him with words of assurance that were unheard and wholly unrealistic. He had never felt so utterly useless in his life as every second passing waiting for assistance seemed like an hour. Gus was lapsing in and out of unconsciousness and Tony simply wasn't sure what was best for him, keep him awake or let him sleep. Does awake mean shock and trauma, does asleep mean the death sleep – he wished he could remember. He tried re-reading his emergency first aid text books in his mind. It was a major relief when he heard the wailing sirens of the approaching ambulance.

Tony stepped back and let the paramedics attend to Gus. Ali arrived at the same time with the Delta 51 crew and immediately went to see Gus as he was being treated by the paramedics. She recoiled in horror as the tablecloth was removed from Gus's leg, but recovered quickly and put her arm around his shoulder, and like Tony tried to reassure him as best as she could in words she struggled to muster. She was politely asked to move back as the paramedics injected morphine and attached an oxygen mask and intravenous drips before carefully placing Gus onto an emergency stretcher.

'We need help to secure the scene Ali, I need to call A.T.O., Scenes of Crime and C.I.D., we need to get North Queen Street to put a guard on Gus at the Mater.......'

'Delta 51 driver will take you back to the station now Tony and get Ronnie up here. You stay in the station and I will get you sorted out, we'll be fine here and Gus will be okay,' Ali said as convincingly as she could.

Tony leaned into the ambulance just before its doors were being shut. The morphine had taken instant and gratifying effect. Gus saw Tony and grabbed him limply around his neck.

'No football for me this Saturday wee man, see you soon eh,' as he drifted off into a drug and shock induced sleep.

'I'll see you later today,' Tony shouted into the back of the ambulance just before the doors were shut and the vehicle left, taking its siren wail with it.

Gus was pronounced dead less than fifteen minutes after arriving at the resuscitation unit of the Mater Hospital in Belfast. Nothing could have saved his life – apart from leaving in place several dirty building bricks.

The Irish Republican Army later issued a statement that the boobytrap had been intended for members of the Orange Order in Carrickfergus who had provoked sectarian unrest by deliberately routing their seasonal band parades and marches past the St Nicolas Catholic Church in the town.

Printed in Great Britain
by Amazon